"I don't want you here, Echo," he said, trying sincerity. "It's too dangerous."

"I know you don't. But you're injured and someone needs to cover your back."

"And that someone is you," he said, and the tone of his voice let her know what he thought of that idea.

"I'm better than nothing," she said, and then added, "Don't say I'm not. You know it's true. If these men are as horrible as you say they are, two people are better than one."

"Not when one of them is a pretty woman," he said, "which is why I'm asking you for the last time to turn the truck around and drive to the airport."

She spared him another glance. "I'm relieved to hear you say this is the last time you're asking. It's getting monotonous. Listen, Adam, I promise I'll go meekly away after this little visit. You'll never have to even think of me again."

He opened his mouth to speak and closed it again without uttering a word. What was the point? He knew he'd never stop thinking about her.

ALICE SHARPE

WESTIN LEGACY

Harlequin®

TORONTO NEW YORK LONDON
AMSTERDAM PARIS SYDNEY HAMBURG
STOCKHOLM ATHENS TOKYO MILAN MADRID
PRAGUE WARSAW BUDAPEST AUCKLAND

This book is dedicated with love and appreciation to my husband,
Arnold, brainstormer superb!

Recycling programs
for this product may
not exist in your area.

ISBN-13: 978-0-373-69576-8

WESTIN LEGACY

Copyright © 2011 by Alice Sharpe

Printed in U.S.A.

ABOUT THE AUTHOR

Alice Sharpe met her husband-to-be on a cold, foggy beach in Northern California. One year later they were married. Their union has survived the rearing of two children, a handful of earthquakes registering over 6.5, numerous cats and a few special dogs, the latest of which is a yellow Lab named Annie Rose. Alice and her husband now live in a small rural town in Oregon, where she devotes the majority of her time to pursuing her second love, writing.

Alice loves to hear from readers. You can write her at P.O. Box 755, Brownsville, OR 97327. An SASE for reply is appreciated.

Books by Alice Sharpe

HARLEQUIN INTRIGUE

746—FOR THE SAKE OF THEIR BABY
823—UNDERCOVER BABIES
923—MY SISTER, MYSELF*
929—DUPLICATE DAUGHTER*
1022—ROYAL HEIR
1051—AVENGING ANGEL
1076—THE LAWMAN'S SECRET SON†
1082—BODYGUARD FATHER†
1124—MULTIPLES MYSTERY
1166—AGENT DADDY
1190—A BABY BETWEEN THEM
1209—THE BABY'S BODYGUARD
1304—WESTIN'S WYOMING‡
1309—WESTIN LEGACY‡

*Dead Ringer
†Skye Brother Babies
‡Open Sky Ranch

CAST OF CHARACTERS

Adam Westin—It's up to him to stop the looting of the prehistoric burial cave located on Open Sky land before an explosive threat from the past destroys everything—and everyone—he loves.

Echo De Gris—She spent her first years of life on the Open Sky. She's back now, but just for a visit. Becoming reacquainted with her childhood nemesis makes her wonder if she'll ever want to leave. A killer makes her wonder if she'll live long enough to get away.

Cody Westin—He's determined not to make the same mistake his father made. He wants his wife back—is he too late?

Brice Westin—Is it true he doesn't know where Adam's mother disappeared to all those years ago, or is it possible he's known all along and will now do anything to protect that secret?

Lonnie Nielsen—He's in for a heap of trouble. Or is he causing it?

Del Halverson—One of Brice's oldest friends. What exactly did he do when he left Wyoming? And is he doing it again?

J.D. Oakes—Another old pal with a hazy past. Is it finally catching up with him?

Pete Westin—Echo's stepfather. Is it a coincidence that he left the Open Sky after Adam's mother's disappearance, and returned the day the violence escalated?

David Lassiter—The cowpoke who ran off with Adam's mother. Or did he?

Willet Garvey—He's no fan of the Westins. How far will hatred and greed take him?

Hank Garvey—Willet's son, Hank is determined to exact revenge at any cost.

Prologue

As Lonnie fumbled the key in the lock, he glanced over his shoulder and scanned the faces of his buddies.

"Remember, you guys," he said, not too surprised to detect a slur in his voice. Damn hooch sure snuck up on a man. "This is top secret. You gotta...gotta promise you won't tell anyone about this. Especially not Janine."

The other two men nodded solemnly.

The key finally clicked and he pushed in the door. He didn't want to turn on the light until he'd secured the room again. Never knew when Janine might take it into her head to come on down to the basement and make sure he wasn't gambling her trust fund away on a busted flush. He urged his friends forward into the heavy shadows. "Don't touch nothing," he warned.

Once they were all crammed inside, he closed the door, slid the dead bolt, switched on the light and waited for a chorus of gratifying gasps.

"What's all this junk?"

The corners of Lonnie's mouth drooped. "What do you mean, what is it? It's artifacts."

"Your 'private stash' is bunch of old broken pots?" one man scoffed. Now Lonnie was getting mad. After all these years he had finally decided to share his collection and this was what he got? He pointed at a square-looking figure in a glass case. "That there, that's a rare Central American Human Effigy. Worth almost five thousand bucks." He pointed at another case. "And that canteen is Southwest Anasazi. I paid three thousand for it. The case over there is full of Mississippian Indian relics. Any museum would love to have just one of these things."

"Where'd *you* get 'em?"

This came from his best friend of the group, who was eyeing Lonnie as though he was some kind of traitor.

"Here and there."

"Black market?"

Lonnie shrugged.

"What about this?"

Lonnie turned to admire a prehistoric carved rock bowl. The handle was a crude rendition of a human head, turned away from the indentation, the skull overlaid with a veneer of gold.

"That's my latest purchase," Lonnie boasted. "It's local, from right here in Wyoming. No one knows which tribe, but it's old. Prehistoric. Paid a bundle for it, too."

"Someone local sold it to you? Who?"

Lonnie shook his head. "No, no, I ain't telling. He promised me more pieces though. Said he was going deeper, whatever that means."

There was a sudden chill in the room as though a north wind had just blown over the top of an icy Rocky Mountain peak. Lonnie looked from one face to the next. Neither set of eyes revealed a thing.

It was there, though. In the air. Something cold and watchful.

He rubbed his eyes, wondering if the booze had made him woolly-headed, but he couldn't shake the feeling he wasn't the only one in that small private room who kept secrets.

Or that the ones he sensed might be as dangerous as his own.

Chapter One

They'd been driving for what felt like forever, but that wasn't the real problem. It seemed to Echo De Gris that her stepfather's anxiety had increased with every advancing mile into Wyoming and now that they were on Open Sky Ranch land, it was almost suffocating.

This made no sense because he was the one who had insisted moving back here soon after Echo's mother's long illness had finally claimed her life. Echo had been surprised when, at the last minute, he'd asked her to come along on the trip—they had never really been close and she was in the middle of life-changing events of her own. But how could she deny him?

"There it is," he said, his voice anxious. He shifted around and flashed her a nervous smile, then peered back out the window. His voice barely a whisper, he repeated himself. "There it is."

She'd been so involved maneuvering the big truck and rented trailer along the gravel road that wound its way through the rolling hillsides of tall grass that she hadn't looked very far ahead. She did now as they topped a peak, and caught a glimpse of a large log house nestled near a pond in the valley below. Aspens surrounded the house while the uncompromising Rocky Mountains ringed the valley. A dozen barns and outbuildings fanned into corrals and fenced pastures while an airstrip ran more or less parallel to a stream. There were several black cows in evidence, their lowing riding on a gentle breeze. Horses, some with foals at their sides, dotted the hillsides.

She'd lived here as a small girl but everything looked bigger now than she remembered. High white clouds, brilliant blue skies, jagged peaks.

And talk about remote…

"Herd must be up at the summer pastures," Pete Westin mused and there was a wistful tone to his craggy voice. She wasn't sure why he'd sold out and moved her and her mother to the West Coast twenty-some-odd years before; she was just grateful he had. Imagine growing up someplace like this. Even the thought of a day or two in such a spot made her itchy.

A few moments later, she drove into the yard, pulling the rig to a stop beside a half dozen other trucks, most of them with dusty ATVs roped into the beds. All she had to do now was help her stepfather get settled, then she was free to catch a ride to Woodwind and buy a ticket on the first plane headed back to civilization.

"I wonder where everybody is. I expected them to be mowing the fields by now, but it doesn't look as though they've even started," Pete said as he opened his door.

Echo scooted out from behind the wheel. "I'll take a look around," she said. It was a big truck with a long drop to the ground and her full skirt caught in the retracting seat belt. She ended up with bare thighs in a swirl of cotton.

"Never mind, here comes someone," Pete called from the other side of the truck.

As Echo battled with her clothes she looked up to see a man approaching.

There was something about a cowboy, even to a city

slicker like her. Maybe it was the snug jeans or the shirt stretched across strong, broad shoulders; maybe it was the way a guy moved when he didn't spend a lot of time sitting. Or the hat—black in this instance—shading the eyes, squaring the jaw. Whatever it was, whew. Some of them just had "it" and you knew what "it" was when you saw it.

He looked away from her predicament, but not before she saw the speculation in his silvery eyes. Damn—she was nearly naked from the waist down. With a final yank, she reclaimed her skirt.

His gaze moved to her face, then away as he appeared to notice her stepfather on the far side of the truck. He looked quickly back at Echo and speculation turned into surprise. "Either Uncle Pete got himself a pretty young wife or you're my little cousin Echo," he said as they shook hands.

She narrowed her eyes and looked him over again. Too young to be Cody…gray eyes…

She'd seen his college graduation picture a few years earlier, taken with his dad, a herd of cattle behind them. "You're Adam," she said.

His smile tipped handsome into gorgeous. "I didn't know you were coming with Uncle Pete."

"It was sort of last-minute. I'll be gone before you know it."

"She's got herself a new job in New York City," Pete grumbled. He'd made no bones about his opinion of her moving across the country.

Adam released her hand. "New York, huh. You've turned into a big city girl."

"I grew up in San Francisco," she reminded him. "I mean, after we left here."

"Well, it's nice to see you. It's been a long time."

"Yes, it has."

Adam continued on around the truck to greet his uncle. "First Pierce comes home and now you. It's getting to be like the old days around here. Welcome, Uncle Pete."

Pete Westin looked genuinely pleased as he delivered a manly clap on the shoulder to Adam. "Where is Pierce?"

"Still in Chatioux. Analise's father took a turn for the worse. They're getting ready to crown her brother king so Pierce extended his stay. He should be home next week."

"I read about what happened here last winter in the newspapers. They made it sound like Pierce was going to marry this Princess Analise."

"That's the rumor."

"How about that? The troublemaker gets himself a princess. How about Cody? Is he around?"

"He and Jamie are working on the mowers. We were supposed to start haying yesterday but everything went wrong. With any luck we start tomorrow bright and early. Dad is out in the barn with a couple cronies you might remember."

"I'll head on out there," Echo's stepfather said.

Adam nodded across the yard. "No need, they're on their way."

Echo turned to see three men. She'd assume she'd recognize her uncle, but the fact was she wasn't sure which of the men was Birch Westin. All three of them appeared to be in their sixties and cut from the same Western cloth, all imposing in their own way, all about the same size. She looked at their hats—the most recent picture she'd seen of her uncle had him in a black Stetson with silver disks on the band. No help there: they all wore tan hats, two of them straw.

That's when she remembered Uncle Birch had had knee surgery last winter followed by a series of setbacks that had delayed healing. One man limped, plus, the closer he got, the more he reminded her of Adam if you looked past the wear and tear of time.

"So, you made it," Birch growled at Echo's stepfather.

Echo's stepfather's shoulders grew rigid. "Yeah," he said.

Birch nodded, then turned to Echo. His voice softened. "This is a nice surprise. I didn't know you were coming, too."

"I'm just here for a day or so," she explained, moving to accept a perfunctory hug. Birch was as stiff a hugger as her stepfather—neither was the warm, cuddly type. Were all the Westin men like that? Her gaze flicked to Adam. Was he?

Birch took up introductions. "Pete, you remember J. D. Oakes," he said, gesturing at the man with the white handlebar mustache and a piercing gaze. J.D. held between two fingers what appeared to be a hand-rolled cigarette. It smelled foul. "And this here is Del Halverson. I don't know if you and Del ever ran into each other way back when."

Pete shook both men's hands. "Sure, I know these two. Del, I think you bought your place a year or two before I left. You'd just returned from the East Coast as I recall."

Del Halverson was a florid man with small features bunched in the middle of a large face. "I wasn't away long," he said. "Got tired of working for my uncle in a damn bank. We all left Wyoming at one time or another, right? Even Lonnie moved away to be a soldier for a while. Big city lights tempt a man. Most of us wander back sooner or later. 'Cept you, J.D. You didn't come from around here."

"I came from a hundred miles north of here. I swear, Del, unless a man is born in your backyard, he's a foreigner." He smiled at Echo as he added, "I remember when you were a wisp of a little girl." Then he dropped his cigarette to the gravel and ground it out with his boot. He looked up, caught Uncle Birch scowling at him, and hastened to pick it up. "Sorry, I forgot," he said, and crossed to an old milk pail filled with sand that leaned beside a post. He dropped in the butt and turned back to Del. "Let's get out of the way so these people can get reacquainted."

Both men said their goodbyes then climbed into one of the trucks and drove off.

An uneasy silence ensued until Echo finally broke it. With a sweeping gesture, she indicated the house. "It sure looks different than I remember," she said.

"Cody remodeled three summers ago before he married Cassie," Adam volunteered.

"Fat lot of good it did him," Uncle Birch snarled. "She ran off last winter anyway."

Echo didn't miss the knot that formed in Adam's jaw. She wasn't exactly sure what prompted it unless he didn't appreciate his father making those kind of comments about his brother.

"This place is hard on women," Pete commented.

Birch turned on his brother. "Is that why you sold me your share of the ranch and moved Althea away? Because the place was hard on her?"

"Partly."

"Pauline is still here," Birch grumbled. "She lasted."

"Maybe because you never married her. Where is she, anyway?"

"In town for the day."

"Looking forward to seeing her. And you know I didn't move just because of Althea. Things weren't the same after…"

His voice trailed off and he looked at the ground.

Birch glowered at his brother. "Go ahead and say it."

The silence that followed his remark was so deep it felt like the earth itself held its breath. Echo shifted uneasily, glancing over at Adam, who was staring at the ground.

Finally, Pete thumped his leg with his fist. "That's all water under the bridge. I'm back now to stay unless you'd rather I didn't. It's not my ranch anymore."

"The Open Sky will always be your home," Birch muttered. "Some things don't change."

"Then take me out to the barn and bring me up to speed. I plan to help with the haying. I used to know my way around a tractor, you know."

A smile lifted Birch's lips for a millisecond. "We can use the help. Come on, Adam, we'll—"

"I can't," Adam said so quickly Echo decided he was as anxious to escape these two querulous old men as she was. He turned to Pete and added, "We discovered someone was looting the burial cave this winter. I need to ride out and check the safeguards Pierce and I put in place. What with haying, there won't be another opportunity for the next few weeks."

Echo saw her chance. "I'll go with you," she said.

"I'm going on horseback."

"That's fine."

"Do you still ride?"

"Of course." *Sort of...*

He glanced down at her sandals. "You're not dressed for it."

"I have boots and jeans in the truck."

"It's a long ride—"

"Oh, come on. I can keep up. I was pretty good on a horse."

"That was a lifetime ago," Adam said.

"I was a natural. Uncle Birch told me so."

Birch actually chuckled as he took off his hat, rubbed the red mark it had left on his forehead and pulled it on again.

"Well, Pete, let's you and me go find Cody and Jamie. Leave these two to pick up where they left off—squabbling." With that, the two older men walked toward the outbuildings, both with ramrod-straight backs, both with hands jammed in their pockets.

Adam's gaze followed his father and uncle.

"So," Echo continued, "are you going to take me with you or not?"

He looked straight into her eyes. "You're as pushy as you were when you were a skinny kid with pigtails."

"I prefer to think of it as highly focused."

"Self-delusional, too," he muttered. "Okay, hurry and change. I'll go saddle a couple horses. You want a broken-down mare or maybe a pony would be more your speed?"

She grinned, pleased he could still dish it out. "Give me a stallion, buddy, I can handle him."

"I bet you can," he murmured as he walked away.

ADAM RODE AHEAD OF THE BLACK gelding he'd saddled for Echo. Bagels was a spirited horse and under normal circumstances, Adam might have chosen another for what he guessed was an out-of-shape rider. But time was short and besides his own mount, Solar Flare, Bagels was the only horse in the barn even remotely suitable.

He smiled to himself at the phrase "out of shape." One look at Echo De Gris in her jeans had confirmed what the earlier glimpse of her bare legs had blatantly announced. Whatever his cousin Echo was, she was also a damn good-looking woman.

Take the glossy short black hair that fell fetchingly across her forehead. Or her black-as-coal eyes, glinting with mischief. Or her slender back and strong arms. Before now his notice of her had been that of a slightly older boy stuck "babysitting" the brattiest little girl in the West. She'd matured into a very attractive woman if you didn't count that willful streak of hers. Look at the way she'd coerced him into this ride.

"Hey up there," she called.

He turned in his saddle to face her and caught a glimpse of her breasts jouncing softly as she rode. Nothing wrong with that, either. "What's up?"

"What's that little yellow building over there?"

"Ice fishing shack. We drag it over the lake when it freezes up, cut a hole in the ice and go to it." He turned in the saddle, but she once again hailed him and he turned back.

"What about that house over there on the point?" She indicated with one hand and swayed slightly in the saddle. The gelding snorted.

"What about it?"

"It looks new. Whose is it?"

"Mine."

"Hold up a minute," she insisted. He rode to the top of the next rise and waited for her.

"I'm in a hurry," he reminded her.

"Then ride, I'll keep up. Tell me about this house of yours. It looks huge. You must be expecting to raise a big family."

He shrugged.

"What's your girlfriend think?"

"I don't have a 'girlfriend.'"

"Don't you like girls?"

"Yes, I like girls," he said. "There's just no one special right now."

"Did you build the house for the one that got away?"

"No one got away," he said, casting her a look. "I haven't met anyone...yet."

"You built the house before you even met a girl you wanted to marry?"

He applied a gentle kick to Solar Flare to increase the speed. Echo did the same to her horse and managed to stay alongside him although her position in the saddle was precarious at best.

"Do you know I produce television shows?" she asked a little breathlessly.

"I thought you were a decorator of some kind."

"Nope."

"Is that your new job in New York, producing television shows?"

"That's it."

"What kind?"

"I did nature shows in San Francisco, but in New York I'm moving to food."

He narrowed his eyes. "What does that mean?"

"I'm going to produce a cooking show. You know, on cable."

"I've never heard of a cooking show," he said honestly.

"You must live under a rock. There are whole channels devoted to cooking and eating and restaurants and all the rest."

He shook his head.

"Anyway," she continued, "last year, in Frisco, we did a three-part special on birds. I produced the segment on Bowerbirds. Have you ever hear of them?"

"I don't think so."

She waved a hand in the air and slipped again, grabbed the saddle horn and steadied herself. The horse tossed his head as if to ask what in the heck she was doing back there. "The male Bowerbirds really go all-out building these fantastic nests to lure a female into mating with them," Echo said a little breathlessly. "Each nest is different, too. The males decorate them with colorful trash they find or maybe with flowers or dead insects…anything to attract a potential partner."

The look he cast her this time was longer. "Wait just a second. Are you comparing me to a bird?"

She laughed. "Judging from that house you're building, you're aiming to capture a princess of your own and raise about ten kids."

"No princess, no thanks. When I marry it will be to a girl who was raised on a ranch and knows exactly what she's in for. And as for kids, don't tell me, let me guess. You don't like them. They're too much trouble. They get in the way of a career."

"Wrong, oh, wise one. I actually like kids." Her forehead creased as she added, "Do you know what all that blustery stuff between my stepfather and your father was about?"

Adam turned away from the lake, following the steep trail into the trees. "It sounded like it was about your mother."

"I think it kind of sounded as though they were talking about *your* mother."

"No," he said firmly. "No one on this ranch talks about my mother."

Echo leaned sideways toward him. When he realized it wasn't entirely on purpose, he put a hand on her shoulder and pushed her back upright.

"Least of all you?" she said.

"Least of all, me."

"But—"

"If your mother had run away with some cowhand

while you were still a little kid, would you have spent a lot of time worrying about her?"

"I guess it would depend on why she ran." Echo gasped as the gelding made a small but jarring leap across a gully. "Understanding that very basic thing seems important to me."

"Not to me."

"My stepfather mentioned your mother sent a postcard after she left. From Canada, I think he said. Did anyone track it down? Why don't you try to find out where she went or if she's dead or alive?"

Reaching the top of the ridge, he once again waited for the gelding to catch up. When Echo was beside him, he met and held her gaze. "Get this straight. My mother died for me a long, long time ago. She chose life with a guy named David Lassiter over a family who loved and needed her. Now, if you want to ride with me, I think we should change the subject, don't you?"

Her black eyes flashed irritation. The gelding, apparently sensing her mood, pawed at the ground and snorted again. "I'm beginning to remember what you were like, Adam Westin. We always had to do everything your way, you always had to be the boss."

"I was older than you." The horse was turning in a circle now, making ominous guttural sounds in his throat. "Echo, be careful—"

"If your whole family is as sanctimonious about your mother as you are, no wonder she ran away!"

"Forget my mother for a minute. Calm down. Your horse—"

"I will not calm down. Maybe the two or three years between us was a big difference when we were little kids, but it's nothing now," she continued. "I have half a mind—"

The horse had had enough. He bolted. Going fast. And in the wrong direction.

Chapter Two

"Whoa," Echo shouted. She yanked on the reins automatically but all that seemed to do was make the horse toss his head. She looked down at the ground and wished she hadn't. A blur of flying hooves, rocks and grass made her dizzy. Any half-baked idea she'd had of abandoning the saddle went away.

Thank goodness the horse had the good sense to stay in the open. At least so far…

Think. No way did she want Adam to save her although it probably beat plunging off a cliff.

Should she try pulling on the reins again? Both reins at the same time? One harder than the other? Help!

She couldn't think straight. Her insides were bouncing around like ice cubes in a cocktail shaker. She was lost in panic mode just like the horse….

So calm him down….

Snatches of long-ago lessons finally fought their way through the electrical flash points in her brain. She needed to center herself in the saddle or she was going to go right over the gelding's head the next time he tossed it. She managed to thread her fingers through a handful of mane down by his withers. Gulping with fear and effort, she attempted what seemed impossible, working to find a rhythm to the horse's thundering gait and adapt herself to it, to stop fighting him. Give him time. All she had to do was stay on his back until he decided he'd had enough.

Gradually it seemed the horse's surges decreased. She gently but firmly squeezed her knees, concentrating like crazy on relaxing into his stride. She was suddenly aware of Adam riding the big red-gold horse alongside her and had no idea how long he'd been there. He didn't try to grab anything, just little by little began backing his horse off and that, too, seemed to reassure the gelding.

At last the gallop became a trot and the trot petered away to a nervous, staccato walk. Echo gently patted the gelding's hot neck and made soothing sounds until he came to a full stop.

Adam slowly got off his horse and took the gelding's reins. She slid out of the saddle. Her knees buckled when her feet hit the ground. Adam caught her and for a few seconds, she leaned against him and breathed heavy.

"Are you okay?" he muttered against her hair.

No voice yet to answer.

"I had no idea Bagels would respond to rider inexperience like that," he said. "You did good, I mean for someone who doesn't know what they're doing."

"The compliments just keep rolling off your tongue," she muttered. Now that it was over, she'd turned into a jellyfish. Eventually it occurred to her that Adam Westin was not stiff like his father or her stepfather, not at all. He was firm and lean, yes, but he was also incredibly tender and his arms supporting her were strong. Warm. Sexy.

She pushed herself away, embarrassed to have such thoughts about him.

He tipped up her chin and smiled down at her. The leap her heart took into her throat was so disconcerting she twisted her head away.

He released her at once. "Take the reins. We'll walk

the horses for a while to cool them off." He smoothed the gelding's long nose. "You okay now, Bagels? Got it all out of your system?"

He started leading his horse up the path and she followed with Bagels, relieved her legs were working again. "I wish I'd known what to call him when he was running off with me," she said.

"I don't think it would have helped."

"Probably not."

They continued on in silence. Bagels pressed his muzzle against her neck every once and a while as though trying to make up and she patted him. The sound of the horses' hooves against the rocks and the birds overhead began to meld together.

The adrenaline rush was gone and now she felt woozy, her feet like granite. "Tell me about this cave we're going to," she called, hoping for a diversion. "For starters, how much farther?"

"Well, you and Bagels very cleverly took us by a different route than the one I had planned," he said, glancing at her over his shoulder, his gray eyes amused. "We'll be coming in the back way now. I guess we'll walk a half hour or so and then ride an hour."

"It's a distance, isn't it?"

"I tried to warn you."

"And when we get there?"

"We check the lock I put on the entrance."

"What exactly was taken?"

"There's no way to know for sure because the contents have never been documented. Apparently, the tribe that used the cave summered here in the high valley. When one of them died, their body was wrapped in blankets and laid to rest inside the cave where there are dozens of fissures. Sometimes amulets or relics of one kind or another were buried with them. My great-grandfather came across the cavern a long time ago and since then, we've all been caretaking it. About thirty years ago, my father made it clear we were all to stay away from it."

"Did you?"

"Not really. My brothers and I just stopped telling him about our adventures. For the most part, we did respect the burial cavern. It was the prospecting shafts we mainly took an interest in, and they're in the main cavern. We didn't advertise our activities to Dad.

"Then last winter Pierce came back to the ranch when Cody was called away and I was hiking in Hawaii. Princess Analise showed up and for some reason they were both pretty vague about, he took her to the cave."

"I read about a cave in the newspaper stories that followed their exploits. The article didn't say anything about burials or relics."

"That's because we kept those facts to ourselves. But at that time, Pierce noticed activity. Since then, I've been keeping a closer eye."

"Are these artifacts valuable?"

He shrugged. "Not overly so, not intrinsically, anyway. Nothing worth a fortune but none of it should have been lost. I've been asking my father to allow me to invite the university in to excavate and preserve the site for years, but he likes things the way they are."

"So it's on Open Sky land?"

"Absolutely. Our family has known about it for generations. I'm surprised Uncle Pete never mentioned it to you."

"Is your father the chatty type?"

Adam laughed. "God, no."

"Neither is Pete. I guess it runs in your family except now that I say that, you can talk when you want to."

His lips twitched and he shook his head.

They climbed a series of rocks, their horses picking their way behind them. Adam turned every so often as if to see if she needed help. She made sure she didn't. Her femme fatale episode was behind her now. Onward and upward.

He was quite a bit ahead of her when she noticed he'd stopped. Shading his eyes with one hand, he was peering up into the sky. "It's getting late," he called. "Let's get to the top of this bluff and ride again. It's a little rocky so go slow."

"Slow is my new middle name," she mumbled, and when she finally returned to the saddle, she did so with a smile on her face if not one in her gut. But Bagels seemed as happy as she was that the drama was over and plodded along behind Adam's mount like a good horse.

"It's over the next ridge," he said at last. They'd actually climbed high enough that snow still existed in shady pockets of land and the temperature dropped. They were soon over the ridge and coming down the far side toward the mountain that was apparently their goal. Echo breathed in big gulps of pine-scented air and marveled that it didn't seem so remote and lonely here after all.

It took her a second to notice Adam had stopped his horse dead in his tracks. She stopped as well, and for a second, admired the way Adam looked sitting in his saddle, the man and the horse in total harmony and striking against the green trees and brilliant blue sky. Eventually it occurred to her there was something ominous in the way he stared down the mountain. He was so still and vigilant....

It began to unnerve her. Even the birds seemed to have stopped chattering in the treetops and both horses stood with their ears perked forward.

Waiting…

Just when she was about to crack, Adam turned toward her. "Someone is down there." His voice was very soft.

The leather saddle creaked as he leaned forward and unsnapped a strap on a long holster that held a rifle, although he didn't take the weapon out of the scabbard.

Okay, this was unnerving. And exciting. Really, she'd been positive she'd die of boredom over the next twenty-four hours and already she'd survived a runaway horse, enjoyed some banter with a good-looking relative and now they were going to catch a grave robber.

"Adam?"

"Shh," he said.

She lowered her voice. "I assume you're talking about a bad guy?"

"I think the odds are pretty good. Come on, stay close to me."

Try to get rid of me….

Maybe instead of cooking shows she should divert into true-life action documentaries. The construction of coq au vin, while interesting, didn't get the pulse pounding like this….

They got off the horses again and walked them partway down the hill. Every twig they trod upon sounded like a thunderclap. Adam finally stopped at a flat spot and tied both horses to a tree. "That looks like an ATV down there. I'm going to check it out. You can stay with the horses."

"That's okay." She fully intended to stay near the gun.

He pulled out the rifle and handled it as though he knew what he was doing. She crept along behind him.

The battered old scooterlike thing sported more rust than paint. It had obviously been parked in an out-of-the-way spot with some attempt at concealment. That kind of shouted nefarious goings-on to Echo, and her spine tingled between her shoulder blades.

He leaned in very close to her, one hand on her shoulder, his breath warm against her ear. The juxtaposition of this intimacy and the tension of the situation really set the sparks flying.

"I'm going to see who's in that cave. I want to catch him red-handed."

Me, too! she thought but didn't say. *No way am I missing this.*

Where was a camera crew when you needed one?

More creeping through the trees until she finally saw where they were headed. Even she could tell the doorlike thing over the mouth of the cave was ajar.

"I'm going in," he said, turning to her. She'd been plastered to his back so they ended up nose to nose. "You stay here. If you hear shots or see someone come running out of that cave, stay hidden behind these rocks. Don't try to help me. Don't try to stop them. Just hide."

"I'm going with you," she said.

"Just listen to me, will you?"

"Stop bossing me around."

"I should have tied you up with the horses." With that he slunk away.

She lost sight of him for a few minutes, then he emerged next to the cave opening. In an instant, he'd slipped inside.

How could she bear standing outside waiting for something to happen? Besides, he might need help.

She started slinking down the trail. When she heard a muffled sound coming from the cave, she broke into a run.

Chapter Three

The lock was neatly sawed in half.

Adam patted his pockets for his flashlight as he stole through the door, then stopped. Whoever was in here had already lit the wall torches. The light wasn't great but it was good enough to make his way.

Last March, Pierce had told him that he had found fuel in the torches which he'd assumed Adam or Cody had put there. They hadn't. After they had proof that the burial chamber had been violated, Adam had made a point of emptying them, but obviously someone had come along after him and filled them again.

Damn. This place was just too remote to adequately safeguard now that someone was intent on robbing it. His father would need to see this for what it was or three generations of Westin stewardship was going to be for nothing. Maybe this thief was going at it slowly, but sooner or later, greed would get the better of him and all this history would disappear forever.

But why now, why after all these years? Who knew about it and how had they found out? Who had told?

Adam paused for a second as a new sound came from the cavern up ahead. It sounded like rocks falling but not enough for an avalanche. Hugging the wall, he waited a few minutes. The sound continued but now he could tell it wasn't falling rocks. He held the rifle down at his side, ready in case he caught someone unprepared and that someone panicked, but not anticipating he would need to use it.

The cave floor was rocky and sloped toward the large main cavern. Two main tunnels led from this cavern; one traveled on to the burial chamber. The other emptied into one of several prospecting shafts.

He paused for a few seconds near the rocks that would give him cover before turning into the main cavern. Then he slowly and methodically rounded the rocks.

The torches had been lit in this cavern, as well. The floor was covered with stalagmites; stalactites descended from the ceiling. This time of year, they dripped steadily, forming rivulets through the main cavern.

A man was working on the distant side, near the outcropping that led to the burial chamber tunnel. He wielded a pickax, apparently breaking up the rocks to create a larger and more direct opening. His movements near one of the torches threw giant wild shadows onto the walls.

Adam's fingers tightened on the rifle. He remembered the metal cart Pierce had discovered in this chamber. They'd talked about what it was used for—neither remembered it being there years before. Now Adam speculated that this man had hauled it here, probably during the winter months when Pierce found the tampered lock on the gate near the BLM lease land. It currently appeared this guy was widening the entrance of the tunnel so he could use the cart for the wholesale looting of the chamber.

Adam swallowed hard. The noise from the man's activities undoubtedly masked Adam's infuriated advance across the cave, but Adam almost welcomed a confrontation. He wanted to know who this bozo was, catch him and haul his ass into town for the sheriff to deal with.

Something of his presence must have filtered through the man's consciousness. The pickax stopped midswing and he turned abruptly. He wore a big tan cowboy hat and a bandana up around his face all the way to his eyes like the old bandits in the television shows wore. Between his getup and the terrible quality of the torch light, it was impossible to tell who he was although he wasn't a huge guy.

None of the Garvey men were very big. Could this be a brother of the late Lucas and Doyle? Since the Garveys blamed the Westins for their deaths, could they feel justified in robbing this cave? No wait, the looting had started before they died. Still, it was possible Lucas had heard something of its existence and passed it along to his family.

"Stop what you're doing," Adam yelled.

The pickax clattered to the rocks, but just as quickly, a shotgun appeared. Adam ducked to the side as a blast whizzed past him. Behind him, he heard a scream.

Adam turned and scanned the cavern as he threw himself behind a forest of stalagmites.

It had to be Echo. He couldn't see her at first because she wasn't at the entrance. She'd traveled halfway around the perimeter of the cavern and was close now to the mine shaft. The thief saw her too and let off a blast in her direction. Echo screamed again and disappeared from sight. The man charged the exit, leaving Adam with a split second to make a decision—he either found out if Echo was hurt or he followed the thief.

He knew what he wanted to do. He also knew what he had to do. With a sinking heart, he kept low but he needn't have bothered—the thief's footsteps rumbled against the earth as he ran up the tunnel toward freedom. Hopefully he'd be so hell-bent on escape that he wouldn't take time to look for their horses. Otherwise, Echo—and he—were in for a long walk home.

ECHO LAY ON HER BACK IN THE pitch-black. Thoroughly winded, she wasn't sure what had happened except she'd fallen, hard, landing on her back, and now was working just to catch her breath.

There wasn't a single inch of her that didn't throb in pain.

And she'd seen Adam so she knew he knew she was there and if she could have heard anything over her own pounding heart and sharp intakes of breath, she imagined it would be him coming to scold her.

That roused her enough to pat the damp ground around her. Rocks, gravel, dirt, some mud...

"Echo?"

Adam. "Did he get away?" Her voice was a croak.

"What do you think?"

A light flashed over her face and she winced. It appeared to originate about ten feet over her head and now that her eyes grew accustomed, she could see she'd fallen down a shaft. To make matters more humiliating, a ladder descended right next to her. Well, if she ever moved again, she could at least climb out of this hole by herself.

Except it wasn't a hole. It was a tunnel. Narrow and shored up with boards, it disappeared into blackness after a few feet. It felt deep and dank and she was sure it was full of unimaginable horrors.

"Are you okay?"

Wasn't that the second time he'd asked her that since they met again? "No," she snapped, but found her breath came a little easier. "I'm fine, really. I'll move in a minute."

"I'll come down—"

"No, please don't. Throw me the flashlight—go after the bad guy."

"Are you sure?"

"Yes."

The light spun toward her and she caught it with one hand by flexing her wrist. Not bad.

"I'll be back very soon," he called but she could already hear his rapid steps leading away from the hole. That was fine with her.

She stayed still for several more minutes, then wiggled various limbs and appendages to make sure everything still worked. Nothing appeared to be broken. Using the sides of the shaft and the ladder, she drew herself to her feet. A quick inspection with the flashlight revealed cuts and scrapes acquired on the way down, rips in her clothing, a little blood and swelling. She took a breath that hurt her ribs, but not as though they were fractured.

Now to climb the ladder.

That took a while, but eventually, she hauled herself out of the shaft and crawled onto the cave floor. Just in time, too, because a tall, dark shape was approaching and she was pretty sure it was Adam.

She sure as hell hoped it was Adam.

"Is that quivering mass of womanhood lying on the floor my little cousin Echo?" he said.

She made herself sit up. "Very funny."

He bent at the knees next to her. "The bad news is he got away. The good news is he didn't have time to scatter the horses so you don't have to walk home."

Instead, she got to ride Bagels the wonder horse who would probably lay back his ears and take off like the wind.

"You're kind of quiet. Hurt anything?"

"Everything. I'm fine, though."

"Good. While you contemplate standing and walking, I'm going to go see what damage that jerk did and figure out a way to keep this place safe tonight."

"Do you know who it was?"

"No." He stood and walked off in the direction the man had been attacking with a pick. She closed her eyes, tried her first actual deep breath and lived through it.

By the time he returned, she'd managed to get to her feet and hobble a ways toward the lighter oval that represented the way out of this cave.

"Find anything?"

He held out his hand. Two charred red shotgun shells rested in his palm. "Aren't you a little glad you fell when you did?"

She swallowed hard. "Yes. Did he take anything?"

Adam extinguished each torch as they left the cave. "The burial chamber looks relatively unchanged from a few weeks ago, but judging from what he was up to today, I think he's getting ready for a major haul."

Limping alongside him, she did what she knew she had to do. "Adam, I'm sorry. If I had stayed outside the cave like you asked me to, you might have found out who he is."

"Hmm," he said, looking down at her. "That thought crossed my mind, too."

"On the other hand if you'd just let me come with you, none of this would have happened."

He didn't answer.

"Do you always have to do everything yourself?"

"Echo, I swear—"

"But it's also possible," she interrupted, "that if I hadn't diverted his attention and drawn his fire, he might have shot at you again. I might have saved your life."

"Honestly. If we weren't related—"

"We're not. Not in any way."

"Well, maybe not technically…"

"Not in any way," she repeated. "If we were, would I do this?" And with that she grabbed his arm, turned him to face her and kissed him.

He backed away at once. "What are you doing?"

"Just what you've been wanting to do since you ogled me in your driveway."

His eyes grew wide, the whites glistening in the poor light. "You are certifiable, do you know that?"

"Maybe I'm just honest."

He shook his head again and clutched her elbow with an iron grip. She would have liked shaking him off, but the support helped. After dousing the last torch in the cavern he spoke again. "So, did you strike gold on your little prospecting tour of the mine shaft?"

"I didn't have time," she grumbled, thoroughly self-conscious now that she'd given in to the impulse to kiss him. She wasn't used to men backing away from her. He was acting like nothing had happened. She knew she should act the same but her pride was a little wounded.

It took a while, but eventually they made it to daylight. It was like being reborn, this coming out of the dark into the light through a small opening, and it felt pretty wonderful. Echo took the deepest breath she'd managed yet.

"How are you going to keep him out?" she asked as he looped the chain through the door.

"I reinforced the burial chamber exit but who knows how long that will work. First things first. You need a medic. Your backside is a bloody mess."

"If I were him, I'd come back tonight while you're all asleep."

"He's not ready yet," Adam grumbled, and she let it drop.

The reality of her backside occupied almost every moment of the long return ride. Thankfully, Bagels plodded along as though bored with the whole thing until he smelled the other horses or recognized the trees—hard to say how he knew they were home, but he did. His pace picked up, she bounced around harder and through it all, clenched her teeth and didn't utter a single sound. By the time she slithered out of the saddle in the ranch yard, she was pretty sure she deserved a Purple Heart.

Pauline appeared on the large porch with a yellow Lab wagging its tail by her legs. Maybe the intervening years had grayed the housekeeper's red curls, but Echo thought she would have recognized her kind face and compassionate eyes anywhere.

Pauline opened her arms as she hurried down the stairs. "Echo De Gris, I heard you were here. Just look at you. You're all grown-up and looking more like your mother, God rest her soul, than ever. Stay down, Bonnie," she added, directing her comment to the dog. To Echo, she added, "Come here, honey."

Echo cautiously shied away from Pauline's hug and the dog's enthusiastic greeting with an apologetic smile punctuated by a wince or two.

"What happened to you?" Pauline demanded, eyes narrowing as she took a good look at Echo's hair and clothes and the smudges and scratches and dirt. "Turn around. Merciful heavens. You're home a few hours and you get yourself all banged up just like you always did. Or did Adam have something to do with this?"

Adam held up both hands. "Don't look at me. Echo still

has a flair for the dramatic. After I unsaddle the horses, I need to talk to Dad. Where is he?"

"Still out working on the mowers with Jamie and Pete and Cody." Pauline waved Adam away and turned her attention back to Echo. "Come along, young lady, we need to get you cleaned up and bandaged before supper, though Lord knows what time of the night those men will actually come in to eat it."

ADAM STOOD AT THE WINDOW and looked out at the moon-drenched silvery landscape. His stomach felt like it was full of snakes and he had his father's obstinacy to blame for it.

He'd moved into his new house when the weather got warm although there was no time to work on fine-tuning the interior and wouldn't be for several months. Nevertheless, he'd hauled in furniture and made himself a home, anxious to be on his own.

Ranching had cycles, all geared to market day in October when the season's calves would be sold. Everything else worked up to and around that. After market, there would still be a million things to do as the winter progressed—fences and machinery maintenance and all the rest required constant vigil. Then they'd move the herd closer to the ranch as calving season approached—the actual grueling weeks of hundreds of cows giving birth, many of them first-time mothers or heifers who needed more help than the experienced animals—followed by moving the herd up to the high pastures for the summer, while mowing the organic grass and hay they would need to feed the cattle when the pastures froze during the winter. Buying good feed because you ran out of your own could eat up profit like crazy.

On and on it went. Since the beef was certified organic,

each animal needed to be cared for in a more hands-on approach; scour and other maladies that befell newborn calves needed monitoring without massive or hit-and-miss doses of antibiotics. It all took extra time.

And his father had agreed to give it an all-out effort, respecting Adam's research and passion about the direction to take with the herd. Adam deeply appreciated this sign of faith.

On the other hand, the old man wouldn't give on the cave. He was stubbornly holding on to the idea that bigger, stronger locks would solve everything and the Westin men could safeguard an extinct peoples' earthly remains forever.

Adam pushed himself away from the windowsill and tried lying down on his new mattress. He was usually comfortable being alone, although tonight he kept thinking about what Echo had said about him resembling a damn Bowerbird. He'd looked it up on the computer after supper—she was right, those birds really went to the extreme. Built elaborate nests for the sole purpose of attracting a sexual mate. Wham, bam, his job was over, the female went her merry way and he waited until the next female bird took a fancy to his nest.

But Adam Westin was not a bird. He was a man and if she couldn't tell the difference—

But he thought she could. There had been a few moments today when he'd felt the overwhelming femininity of her colliding against him; he'd had to force himself to remember this wasn't another pretty girl, this was his uncle's stepdaughter. Worse, she was a television producer. What in the hell did a cowboy and television producer have in common?

How about that kiss?

No, she hadn't meant that. She was just toying with him. She liked to make him squirm, that's all that was.

He was soon back at the window, fidgeting with the blinds he'd installed, thinking maybe if the room was darker—

What had Echo said? Something about how if she was the looter, she'd come back tonight.

What did she know?

He heard a far-off motor, thought he saw indistinct shapes moving through the trees; it even looked like a horse was down there on the far side of the lake.

He rubbed his eyes and shook his head and everything disappeared except the feeling that he shouldn't be locked inside this house, he should be at that cave. If Echo was right, he'd never forgive himself....

Or her, for that matter.

Fifteen minutes later, dressed and armed with his trusty hunting rifle, he rode out of his barn.

Chapter Four

He skirted the calm lake, traveling the moonlight-dappled trail at a steady gait. Now that he'd made the decision to go, he cursed the hours he'd wasted after their late supper.

Echo hadn't shared the male-only meal. Pauline explained she and Echo had eaten hours earlier and Echo had begged off visiting that night in favor of nursing her wounds. He would have liked to see her—since the moment he'd left her side, she'd been ever present in his mind. He found her combination of audacity and humor both annoying and interesting. The Westin household could at times be pretty darn somber.

There'd been a couple of years when things had been different at the Open Sky. Right after Cody married Cassie and brought her home, every corner of the big place had suddenly filled with light. Cassie was a beauty with tumbling fair hair and angelic blue eyes, and the way she and Cody had looked at one another had made Adam curious about the kind of love that blossomed into a lifetime promise. He'd enjoyed their interactions, he'd been amused by his father's more frequent smiles. Cassie even managed to win over Pauline who was pretty damn territorial when it came to her kitchen and household. But Cassie was like that. Easy to like, full of kindness.

At least at first. And then she'd grown increasingly

quiet and concurrently, Cody had retreated inside himself. It was obvious their marriage was in trouble.

It culminated at last in a macabre reenactment of the past. Cassie left the ranch just as Adam's mother had done decades before her. At first it had seemed she'd just be gone a few days, but time had passed and she'd just not come back.

Afterward? After Cassie left? It was obvious to Adam that Cody was determined to find her. Maybe it was because their father hadn't tried to find their mother that he became obsessed with it. He'd hired a detective he thought no one knew about, and Adam was pretty sure it was a call from that detective that had made Cody call Pierce home months before.

Love hadn't been kind to the Westin men, although Pierce swore his own tragedies that had included a ruined marriage had lifted the moment he met Princess Analise Emille. Adam hoped the passion he saw between them would burn forever; it worried him that his brother had chosen to share a ranching life with a woman raised in a castle of all places....

And yet she seemed tough under all that refined glamour, and very sure of what and who she was. What more could anyone give than the truth of their essence?

Careful, he warned himself. *You don't want to become one of those damn cowboy poets.*

He urged the horse onward. Solar Flare knew the trails as well as he did—both of them could travel in near dark. Without Echo and Bagels to create a diversion, the route they traveled was a lot faster. Within an hour he was close enough to the cave to slow down lest thundering hoofbeats alert someone—if anyone was out here to alert.

Solar Flare appeared to understand the concept of tiptoeing or so it seemed to Adam as he led him along the path. The valley where a long-extinct Native American tribe had presumably summered hundreds of years before was full of shadows; the cave mouth was a short climb up the mountain face and, as luck would have it, located on the side of the mountain illuminated by the moon.

Still, unfortunately, it was impossible to tell if the covering door to the cave stood ajar. Too many shadows. He'd have to go up there and look.

He tied Solar Flare to a tree before proceeding down the hillside toward the valley. His plan was to skirt the flat areas and climb the mountain hugging the shadows. This time he'd have his rifle ready.

If the lily-livered thief was currently inside the cave busily looting his greedy little heart out, maybe there was a better way of catching him, one that wouldn't result in more gunfire. How about guarding the cave entrance, calling Cody on his cell to get together a few guys and come on out here? Call the sheriff, too. Hell, the more the merrier.

On the other hand, the very act of disturbing the artifacts was a sacrilege and if left to do as he pleased, the thief would undoubtedly strip the burial cave clean before daybreak. He might not get out if Adam guarded the door, but the damage would be done.

A movement in the bushes ahead settled matters. The thief apparently hadn't made it to the cave yet. If Adam could get the drop on him, he could launch a surprise attack and bundle the culprit off Open Sky. By dawn he'd be back to work and this would be over with.

All these thoughts raced through Adam's mind as he crept down the dark side of the hill, glad the moonlight wasn't directly overhead to give away his position. Every few seconds he stopped to listen, alarmed when he no longer heard movement. Had the thief detected Adam's approach?

The question was answered an instant later when Adam felt the barrel of a gun jab into the middle of his back. Damn, he'd been made.

"Drop the rifle."

The voice was muffled. Adam flashed on the bandana the thief wore over the lower part of his face; that explained the voice....

"I said drop it."

Adam slowly lowered the rifle to the ground at his side. When the thief unexpectedly leaned over to pick it up, Adam seized the moment. Turning on the balls of his feet, he tackled the man.

Clutched together, they tumbled down the sloping land, Adam's rifle abandoned behind. The guy wasn't very big or strong though he threw some decent punches and with both hands, which meant he must have lost his weapon, too. After a few moments of wrestling and grunting, Adam pinned the guy to the ground and sat on him, keeping a forearm across his throat. They were both breathing heavy.

Gradually, it occurred to Adam that something was wrong.

He tried to blink into focus the pale oval face beneath his but the light was miserable. He felt for the bandana but it must have come off in the struggle and his fingers grazed slick lips. The click of teeth warned he'd come close to getting bitten. He loosened his stranglehold. "Who the hell—"

"Are you trying to kill me?" his victim demanded.

"Not yet. Not until I find out who you are."

There was a long pause followed by a whispered, "Adam? Is that you?"

A waft of some kind of fruity scent hit his nose at the same time he realized the slippery substance he'd felt on his fingertips was lipstick. Echo!

How could he have not known he was sitting on a woman? Now that he did, everything about her was obvious, from her breasts pressed between his knees to the softness of her throat under his fingers…

He drew both hands back. "Are you okay?"

"*Please* stop asking me that."

"Maybe if you could go more than a couple hours without throwing yourself under a bus, I would."

"Move. You're heavy."

"I don't know if I should. You're a walking, talking menace." He said this as he moved off her. On his knees by her side, he offered a hand, which she must have seen as she took it. They sat face-to-face in the dark.

He took a deep breath. "What are you doing out here?"

"The same thing you're obviously doing."

"But you were injured."

"Pauline is a whiz with bandages and antiseptic."

He shifted his weight off a sore leg. "Why in the world did you think it was a good idea to jab a gun against my spine?"

"I thought you were the bad guy. You were making a lot of noise—"

"I was not."

"Oh, please. How do you think a greenhorn like me managed to get the drop on you?"

"Judging from everything I've seen since you got here, I'd say dumb, blind luck."

"You wish."

"Where did you get a gun, anyway?"

She was quiet for a second. "Well, it wasn't really a gun."

"I'm almost afraid to ask."

"It was a stick."

"You stuck a stick in an armed man's back?"

"More like a branch. I thought you were *his* partner..."

Adam's heart skipped a beat. "*His* partner? Whose partner? You mean you saw someone else out here?"

"Yes. I think—"

Her voice broke off as he grabbed her arm and hauled her to her feet. "Where?" he insisted. "When?"

"On the mountain, right before I heard you coming."

"At the cave?"

"He was climbing...."

He dropped her arm. "And then you and I made a huge ruckus fighting our way down the slope. He couldn't have missed hearing that."

"I suppose—"

"Which means he'll come investigate."

The flare of her sudden anxiety charged the still air between them like a downed electrical wire. Her voice dropped to a whisper. "Maybe he'll just leave."

"Maybe not."

"Let's go find your rifle."

"My idea exactly." When their hands brushed, he grabbed her fingers. Best to keep her close so she didn't go off on a tangent and get them both killed.

They climbed the slope as quietly as they could, stopping every few feet to feel for signs of broken bushes to confirm they were going the right direction. The light was slightly brighter headed uphill; a flashlight would have helped a lot but no way was Adam going to risk that.

"I need both hands," she whispered, and broke away. After a few seconds during which he came across his jack-knife which must have tumbled out his pocket unnoticed, she added, "I found the branch I used. Your rifle has to be somewhere nearby."

The words had no sooner passed her lips when gunfire sounded from the valley and a piece of the bark—on a tree less than five feet away from Adam's head—flew off and hit him on the cheek. The gunman had found them in the shifting moonlight. Even Adam could see Echo down on all fours patting the ground. Just as she found his rifle, another shot sounded.

"Stay down," he hollered right before the impact of a bullet spun him to the ground. He grabbed his left shoulder. Blood seeped through his fingers. "Echo! Where are you? Find cover!"

He lay still, hoping she hadn't been hit, as well. She'd been up the slope, behind him, but he couldn't locate her exact whereabouts now without sitting up and he wasn't going to do that.

And then he heard noise. Steps, breaking plants, broken twigs… Someone was coming up the hill toward them.

"Stop right there!" Echo hollered, her voice closer than Adam had figured. "Stop or I'll shoot." Without waiting, she let loose with the weapon.

The noise was deafening. Adam squeezed himself into the ground, willing himself to shrink and praying Echo kept the gun barrel high enough to miss him. He could imagine how terrified she was—damn, he was just as terrified but mostly of her.…

He closed his eyes. If the unknown gunman kept advancing while being on the receiving end of Echo's volley, he couldn't be too big a chicken.

It seemed to go on and on in a distant fading way. Adam felt himself drifting. He was glad for the warm earth beneath him as hell raged overhead.

Chapter Five

She moved her hands over his prone body and felt blood and torn clothes.

Tears sprang to her eyes as she leaned over him and whispered his name, feeling his throat, searching for a pulse, cursing herself for becoming a television producer when she could have done something useful with her life like going to medical school. She felt no reassuring pulse, just the shaking of her own hands.

The moon bathed his face in silver light, glancing off the planes of his cheeks, stressing his bone structure. His hat was long gone and his hair now brushed his forehead above his eyebrows. He looked young and vulnerable, more like the child she'd known a lifetime before, the one she'd worked hard to impress or infuriate, anything but be ignored....

Smoothing a few dark locks away and leaning down, she carefully kissed his lips. "I'm so sorry—"

A hand clutched her wrist and she gasped.

"What are you sorry about now?" Adam mumbled.

She threw herself down on him, tasting the salt from her own tears as she kissed his face a half dozen times.

"Easy, easy," he said, his voice soft. "I'm fine. Just a little bullet hole. Where's the gunman?"

She sat back up, wiping tears away from her cheeks,

gathering her aplomb. "I heard an engine start," she said at last.

"And you're not hurt?"

"No, I'm fine. Just scared. I thought you were dead and I thought it was my fault, that my bullets had hit you. Damn it, Adam, I thought I killed you!"

"I'm sure you tried your best," he said, releasing his hold on one of her hands. "The other guy just got me first. Help me sit."

She smiled at his snarky remark, feeling better at once. The world was whole again. "Do you think sitting is a good idea?"

"Yeah. Come on, help me."

She gave him a hand to steady himself as he slowly sat up. She'd brought along a flashlight and she used it now to study his wound, poking with her finger a little. He shrank away from her.

"You're kind of delicate for a cowboy, aren't you?" she asked.

"Watch it!"

"I don't think the bullet is still in there. I think it went right on through."

"This is your expert opinion?"

"Yes. I gave my cat a distemper shot once. I know all about this stuff. I'll stop the bleeding and you'll feel better."

Within a few minutes, she'd stripped off her jacket. She was about to tell him to close his eyes but that was silly. Without a flashlight pointing at an object—in this case *her*—it was darn near invisible. She pulled the sweatshirt over her head, then put the jacket back on over her bra.

The sweatshirt got cut into a dozen strips and patches with his pocketknife. "It's not bleeding too much anymore," she finally said as she tied the last soft strip of cotton around his shoulder. "Did you ride your horse?"

"Yeah. How about you?"

"I brought Bagels."

"After what you went through today, you saddled Bagels and rode him all the way out here?"

"Yes. All by myself." She didn't mention getting lost once or twice. No need for details.

"I doubt he's still around."

"I don't know. I tied him up pretty good."

"Judging from the way he reacted to your tension earlier today, the gunfire must have terrified him. Don't worry, he'll find his way home, but it means you're stuck here with me because I'm not leaving this cave. Will you dig my phone out of my left pocket?"

"You can't stay here!"

"I'm not leaving."

"I'll stay, you go home."

He laughed—oblivious in the dark of her narrowing eyes—but his voice, when he spoke, was soft. "Please, Echo, just help me get the phone."

She did as he asked, squeezing her hand into his front left pocket. It was a tight fit and she could tell her hand fishing around down there had a predictable effect on his libido, which was pretty amazing given his current condition. She tried to make the search as impersonal as possible. Still, his arousal intrigued her—perhaps he wasn't indifferent to her, after all. Hooking his phone, she dragged it out of his pocket and handed it to him. "Who are you calling?"

He wouldn't meet her eyes. "Cody. He can come help us so we can go back to the ranch. I need to make arrangements to have this site protected."

"But your father—"

"To hell with my father. You could have been killed tonight."

She diplomatically chose not to point out that she wasn't the one with a bullet in the shoulder. Instead, she cleaned up the makeshift medical supplies while Adam called his brother. As he talked, she went downhill in search of Bagels and found he'd bolted just as Adam had predicted, all but breaking off the limb to which he'd been secured. Then she marched uphill and found Adam's horse quietly munching weeds and staring into the dark as though this was just a night like any other.

But it wasn't.

She leaned her forehead against the big horse and wrapped an arm around his neck. He produced a soft sigh and nuzzled her hair.

Eventually she wandered back to Adam's side and found he'd scooted up sideways to lean against a tree. A quick once-over with the flashlight revealed he was ashen beneath his tan and his teeth were clenched.

"Cody is on his way," he said.

She sat down beside him. "How are you doing?"

"Peachy."

"How are you really doing?"

"Nothing I can't handle."

"Are you cold?"

"A little. You?"

"Yes," she said although she wasn't. All that running up and down the hill had warmed her up, but he looked like he could use a little TLC. She moved closer, snuggling against his right side and doing her best to remember she was there for warmth and comfort and nothing else.

"I have to hand it to you," she said.

He'd sunk down a little. "Why?"

"Well, I thought life on a ranch would be kind of, I don't know, predictable."

"It is," he murmured.

She didn't respond. Nothing she'd experienced since getting here had seemed even remotely predictable.

In a halting voice, he added, "Normally it's all about the ranch. The cows. The animals. Things happen in a pattern, seasons bring different challenges. Pulling calves—"

"What's that mean?"

"Helping the mother give birth. Anyway, nothing that's gone on today has anything to do with ranching."

She leaned closer until their heads touched. He didn't draw away. "So this isn't another day at the office?"

"No," he murmured.

They sat quietly until she noticed his breathing had grown deeper and his weight against her arm heavier than before. "Adam?" she whispered.

No response. For a second her heart froze—what if he'd gone unconscious or even died? Then he made a soft groaning noise. Just asleep. That meant it was up to her to keep watch. Sitting as still as she could, she concentrated on night noises and was astounded by how many of them there were.

What would she do if she suddenly heard the sound of a returning motor? There was no more ammunition. The concern had no sooner sprung to mind than it turned real.

"Adam," she said again, this time more urgently.

He jerked awake. "What?"

"I hear an engine."

He tilted his head and listened. "Relax, it's coming from the lake trail and our thief comes around from the mountain. It must be Cody."

She took a deep breath and got to her feet, hoping he was right.

By the time Cody appeared, his vehicle's headlamp sweeping the clearing, she'd collected Solar Flare and helped Adam stand.

Cody was slightly taller and heavier than Adam, good-looking as all the Westin men were, in an outdoor tough-as-nails way. Where Cody differed the most from Adam were his eyes. It wasn't only that they were darker. It was the No Trespassing sign that was impossible not to notice. She knew his marriage had fallen apart several months earlier, but really, in this day and age, besides Adam, who hadn't suffered that fate? She herself had been in and out of different relationships for years, even tying the knot once for a whole eleven months.

"Hello, Echo," Cody said as he got off the vehicle, produced an electric lantern and held it aloft. "I was hoping to see you again before you left, but not like this. Are you okay?"

It was like the Wyoming question of the day. "Fine," she said. "It's your brother who's about to drop."

Cody directed the light and looked at Adam closely. He whistled. "Man, you look like hell."

"I feel like hell."

"You want to carry that bullet back to the ranch or do you want me to dig it out here?"

"*Dr. Quinn, Medicine Woman* here says the bullet isn't in there."

Echo rolled her eyes.

"You were lucky you weren't up here alone when that happened," Cody said.

Adam's fingers grazed Echo's arm. "I know." His attention once again on Cody, he added, "Sorry I had to wake you."

"You didn't wake me. The two oldest Garvey brothers showed up at the house about an hour and a half ago, drunker than skunks. They swear Open Sky owes them two hundred bucks in Lucas's back wages."

"They were both there?"

"In the flesh."

"Damn."

"Are you sorry you missed them?" Cody asked with what Echo suspected was a rare flash of a smile.

"No, I just had my heart set on one or both of those losers being behind the thefts and this shooting. If they were at the ranch yelling at you, they weren't out here shooting at us."

"Back to square one."

"So, despite the fact Lucas did his best to kill Analise and Pierce, his brothers want money."

"That's right. I'm about ready to pay them out of my own pocket and get rid of them for good."

"I'll go half with you."

"Deal. You'd better get back to the ranch. I'll take Solar Flare up to the cave and keep guard. I'll come join the mowing as soon as Mike relieves me in the morning."

"I can run a tractor," Adam said.

"Maybe."

During the ensuing pause, Echo had to keep her mouth clamped shut. It was second nature to offer help, but she'd never even ridden in a tractor; on the other hand she had mastered her stepfather's truck—how hard could a tractor be?

However, that wasn't the plan. Tomorrow she was figuring out how to get to the airport and return home just to pack her bags and fly to New York where she had a month to find an apartment and learn to navigate the city before she started work. Time to let go of the past, the mountains and Adam Westin.

"I'm calling the university in the morning," Adam

finally said. "If they can start processing the cave this summer, they can figure out how to guard it."

He and Cody exchanged long glances, which Echo assumed had something to do with the fireworks they knew would ensue once their father got wind of their plan. With any luck, she'd miss it.

Cody gave her a few quick instructions on how to run the ATV and Echo and Adam took off.

ADAM LOVED THE SIGHT OF acres of windblown rolling grass in the early morning light. It was a sea of green and gold, peaceful and vast as seen through the windshield of the tractor. Mowing it down was an almost hypnotic experience, mind-numbing in its repetitive nature and yet oddly satisfying, as well.

Usually, that is.

Not today. Today his shoulder reminded him of the night before and the night before was disturbing for a host of reasons.

He'd been at it since right after dawn, which meant precious little sleep but that wasn't what had his gut in a knot. Jamie had assured him Echo was right, there was no bullet lodged in the flesh, but he would still need to drive into town and have the doctor take a look at it for insurance purposes. As Echo needed a ride to the airport that afternoon, it seemed natural that he should take her along. She was leaving.

But that wasn't what made him antsy, either. He looked up at the blue sky and a circle of vultures spiraling a mile or so away and felt cold. He kept mowing.

At eleven-thirty he returned to the field closest to the road where he'd made plans to meet Echo. Cody had showed up as well, as had their father. Pete and Jamie must be off in different fields, maybe miles away.

Adam cleaned himself up with the help of spring water while his father fooled with his tractor, which was apparently acting up, and Cody sat in the shade of his rig eating a sandwich. He offered Adam lunch, but Adam declined. He was entirely too anxious to eat.

He was relieved when his pickup rolled onto the field, Echo behind the wheel. She was right on time.

All night long, he'd thought about her, reliving her fervent kisses, reviewing each acerbic word she'd uttered. She was not his kind of girl and yet there was something about her that had begun to worm its way under his skin. He was glad she was leaving the ranch. He didn't want to think about her anymore.

As the truck stopped a few feet away, he caught sight of Cody waving him over. Bonnie had stretched out in the shade beside him. Her tail thumped once or twice when she saw Adam.

Cody handed him a thick envelope. "You'll be going right by the Garvey place. Stop by and give them this. I wrote up a paper and everything so it's all formal. This is what we technically owed Lucas at his time of death. There's no more. Tell them if they come again, we'll charge them with trespassing."

"Got it. I'll go to the bank and get out enough to pay you back my half. I assume we're not telling Dad."

Cody almost shuddered. "God, no. Did you call the university?"

"I emailed the department head a few weeks ago. She was very receptive and then Dad blew up and I backed down. I emailed her again this morning but I haven't had a chance to see if she responded yet. Thought I'd drop by on the way to the airport and talk to her personally."

"My plane leaves at six twenty-five," Echo said. Adam hadn't realized she'd approached. He turned to assure her that he'd have her there in plenty of time but for a second, his vocal cords froze.

She was wearing a fitted black jacket over tailored white jeans, a wispy black-and-white blouse underneath, bold silver earrings and slicked back hair, red lips. The look was anything but random or casual. Her shoes were city bound and how she kept the tapered heels from sinking into the ground was a mystery. She looked sophisticated and classy in a way few women he had occasion to see in person ever looked.

And like a stranger. He could no more imagine the woman standing in front of him on a runaway horse or lying in the bottom of a mine shaft than he could picture her snuggling against him when he was hurt let alone covering his face with relieved kisses. Even her dark eyes held an edge they hadn't shown before.

"Adam, wait a second," Cody said softly as Echo made her way to say goodbye to Birch. He lowered his voice. "Did you tell Dad about last night?"

Adam tore his gaze away from Echo's shapely retreating form and looked down at his brother. "Not yet."

"Me neither."

"I asked Jamie to keep it to himself, too. I'll come clean tonight when it's a done deal. He can throw a fit then for all the good it's going to do him."

"You sound just like him."

"I think I'll take that as a compliment."

Cody smiled. "Might as well."

Adam knelt down, balancing his butt on his heels so he could lower his voice. "Yesterday in the cave, the looter's shot was so wide that at the time, I thought he was just trying to scare us into hiding so he could get away. But last night's attempt was brazen. He was coming up that hill as though he was going to make a kill. For some reason, things escalated. He's not going to stop this until we make him stop."

Cody held up both hands. "You get no argument from me."

"Yeah, well, Dad knows most of what's going on, too, and yet he puts up roadblocks and waxes poetically about Westin responsibility. Why?"

Cody's eyes narrowed. "What are you getting at?"

Adam stared hard at his brother, then shook his head. "I don't know what I'm getting at. But I'm not taking no for an answer. Not this time. I'm not willing to risk my life or anyone else's life for a bunch of old bones. What I don't get is why Dad is."

He got to his feet abruptly as he spied Echo approaching. He felt an uneasiness he'd experienced just a few times in the past; things were running on an agenda he couldn't see or understand—yet.

"Ready?" she asked Adam as she shook Cody's hand goodbye.

Adam took out his cell phone. "You drive. I have a call to make."

Chapter Six

He checked his email as she drove, then called Mike who reported he'd heard the sound of a distant engine about an hour before. One blast from his shotgun had apparently alerted whoever was approaching that the cave was guarded and the noise had retreated. Adam repeated his directions to Mike to take no chances. He hung up, the anxious feeling worse than ever.

"Will they finish up without you?" Echo asked as she accelerated up the hill.

"Finish what?" he said, jerking around to look at her.

"The mowing. Seeing you all in the field today made me wish I was still working in Frisco. Your ranch would make a great Americana show. Everywhere I looked, there was a picture that seemed to tell a story. That's the best part about producing television, you know, when what you film opens doors to reveal glimpses of something else."

He looked at her distinct profile and couldn't help but think how lovely she was. And smart. And frustrating. And totally wrong for him.

"Well, I don't know about all that," he said, "but the mowing will take several days. There are other pastures besides this one. The mown grass has to dry before we can bale it and then it needs to be hauled and stored—the process takes most of a month."

"This is what you meant yesterday when you told me ranching was predictable."

"Precisely. Not that emergencies don't arise that require a change in plans, but generally speaking there are things that have to be done no matter what."

"The same is true in any profession," she said.

He nodded. He imagined it was. He just couldn't quite equate the importance of creating a TV show with the life-and-death struggle of ranching, but he supposed that was because he was kind of biased. The thought of spending his life inside four walls all day made him squirm.

He turned when they passed the Garvey place, straining to see if anyone was home. The usual menagerie of old cars and trucks decorated the fenced yard—impossible to tell if anyone was there, but in all likelihood one or more of them would be. He needed to figure out the right approach....

"What were you looking at?" Echo asked as they sped down the road.

"We just passed the Garvey place."

Her foot let up on the gas pedal. "Shall I turn around?"

"No."

"But I thought I heard you tell Cody you'd stop by and talk to them."

He hoped that was all she had heard. "Not with you along," he said adamantly.

There was a deep silence followed by a swift glance, narrowed eyes and a muttered, "You know, not everything that happened yesterday was my fault."

He shook his head. "That's not what I meant. These men are thugs. Hard drinking, hard living, in and out of jail and trouble. Two of them were murderers and the ones who are left detest every Westin on the planet. I just don't want to subject you to them, that's all."

She gave him a longer glance this time, her dark eyes intense. "I understand," she said at last, and damn if he didn't miss her taking another jab at him. This Echo De Gris was like the physical twin of the one he'd met yesterday, and he wondered what had happened to change her in just one night.

Why couldn't he stop thinking of her lips on his face, of the whiff of perfume he'd inhaled and subsequently followed into consciousness? She was just another woman and as poor a match for him as anyone could dream up, but he kept having to fight the urge to shake her new cool veneer and rattle her the way she'd rattled him.

He had her stop at the bank to get his share of the money he owed Cody, then they proceeded to the university. The campus was located on the outskirts of town. Adam knew exactly which building to park next to thanks to his former research. As he'd told Cody, he'd sent an email that morning to Dr. Wilcox who was the head of the archaeology department. On the way into town, he'd checked his email from his phone and was relieved to find she'd be in her office and was still very interested in his proposition.

"You can take a cab from here if you like," Adam told Echo after she'd parked the truck. "It's not that far."

"Why would I do that?"

"I just thought it might be easier for you than waiting around for me."

"If you don't mind, I'll come with you," she said.

"Since when do you care if I mind?" he asked with a grin.

His joking fell flat in a way it wouldn't have the day before. Unsure how to fix it, he jerked his head. "Come on. It wouldn't be the same without you."

"No, maybe you're right." She was digging in her large

handbag and finally produced a cell phone. "I'll call a cab company. Better get used to it, right? That's how I'll be getting around in New York. I won't have a car—"

"What's wrong with you?" he interrupted.

A familiar flash ignited her eyes. "Nothing is wrong with me."

"Something is wrong. You're all standoffish."

"And you're all tense."

"Okay, I'll give you that."

She shook her head. "Listen. We're wasting time."

"Will you be here when I get back?"

She took a big step toward him and stuck out her hand. "I'll take care of myself. It was great seeing you, Adam. Thanks for the adventure."

He took her hand and they shook, but when she tried to draw away, he pulled her against him, careful her weight landed against his good shoulder. Tossing common sense aside, he lowered his voice to a whisper. "My turn to say goodbye." Without allowing himself one more rational thought, he kissed her.

She gave a halfhearted push, which he ignored. He'd intended the kiss as payback for the day before, but the second his lips touched hers that notion went out the window. She trembled as she melted into him. She had the softest lips in the world and the invitation buried in her kiss sent spikes of desire racing through his groin that were so strong they hurt.

She broke their connection. Her eyes were huge and soft and she looked as disheveled now as she'd looked pulled together a minute before.

"Adam—"

He kissed her again, quickly this time. He could have kept at it all day, but he was suddenly aware of a whole bunch of things including two white-haired men who had stopped to chuckle.

"Goodbye," Echo said, and this time she kissed his cheek. She slapped his arm in a parody of the many good-old-boy greetings she'd undoubtedly witnessed in the past twenty-four hours but unfortunately, she chose the wrong arm and he winced. "Oh, sorry," she said, her forehead wrinkling with concern, but it was soon gone. "Take care, Adam," she added, and grabbed her suitcase from the back of the truck. She took off down the sidewalk at a fast clip, her heels punctuating her steps with sharp retorts, her phone held up to her ear.

He turned and walked the other way.

Dr. Wilcox was an attractive woman hovering near forty with chocolate-brown skin and hair and eyes to match. She wore loose-fitting khaki jeans and a matching shirt; it appeared that, with the addition of a pith helmet, she'd be ready to start a dig that very afternoon.

"I can't tell you how excited we are about this," she said, perching on the edge of her cluttered desk, square brown hands waving as she spoke. "I was so disappointed when your father backed out earlier this year, but this is just perfect."

Adam stood a few feet away, supporting his left arm with his right hand. Echo's parting gift had jarred his injured shoulder and the throb was back. "Why perfect?"

"Because we have a visiting archaeologist who will be here for four weeks and I was hoping I'd have something as fascinating as ancient remains to interest him. Your burial cave sounds perfect. I've already talked with Professor Lavel. We'd like to bring out some graduate students tomorrow and take a look, start a survey, get things rolling. Your father is ready to sign the papers this time, right?"

"He'll sign," Adam said firmly.

She popped to her feet. "Wonderful!" Walking quickly around the desk, she chose a large manila envelope from the pile teetering atop a file cabinet and handed it to Adam. "I've earmarked all the appropriate spaces so it's pretty self-explanatory, but call if he has questions. I wrote my number in there at the top. We'll stop by the ranch at 6:00 a.m. unless that's too early."

"That's fine. By then I'll be mowing but I'll keep an eye out for you. And as I said in the email, there's a looter at work so you need to enact security measures. He even took a few shots at us yesterday, so please be careful."

"We know how to deal with this kind of situation. It calls for speed but not at the expense of methodical procedure. What we have that you probably lack is manpower— lots of enthusiastic students. We'll keep the place so busy no one will have a chance to create problems."

"Then I'll see you tomorrow. Will you need all-terrain transportation or—"

"No, no, we'll bring our own equipment. All we need from you is an introduction to the site." She tapped the envelope. "And permission to excavate."

"Then I'll see you tomorrow."

They shook hands, and Adam left feeling slightly better. Of course the relief was tempered by the fact he would need to get his father's signature on the right forms; he was sure he could do it when he related the events of the previous evening.

But the knot was still there. The ominous feeling, as dark as a winter sky creeping over the Rockies, just wouldn't go away.

He was barely out of the building when his truck appeared at the curb, Echo behind the wheel. Surprise, surprise.

He got in the passenger seat and turned to look at her. "What are you doing here?"

She looked away from him as she pulled onto the quiet street. "I have hours before my plane departs. The taxi would have cost thirty dollars. I'm cheap."

"You should have left," he said, buckling his seat belt. "It's time for you to get on with your life."

"Oh, please," she said, her voice sharp. "Stop preaching at me. You sound just like my stepfather."

"I'm only pointing out the obvious."

"You're being obnoxious. I'm a grown woman. I can take care of myself."

"Damn, you're a spoiled brat sometimes."

"Just sometimes?"

"Some men like the spitfire type."

"I take it you don't."

"Overrated." He took a deep breath and chided himself for getting into it with her. Big deal, she was cheap. Airport, doctor, Garvey place, home. Then a big old dust-up, get a signature, done. One thing at a time. He took a few deep breaths.

They drove through the campus in silence, but when they reached the exit, she turned back toward the ranch.

"Hey, you're going the wrong direction," he said, searching for a good place where she could turn around.

This time she glanced at him as she spoke. "No, I'm not. Like I said, I have hours to spare and you need to talk to those Garvey men."

"I told you—"

"I know what you told me, but to heck with that," she said, accelerating as the speed signs indicated.

"Wait a second," he growled. "I will not take you to the Garvey house. Period."

"You're forgetting who's driving the truck."

"And just exactly *how* is that? Where did you get the keys?"

"I never gave them back to you."

So that's why she'd hung around, to return his keys. "I don't want you here, Echo," he said, trying sincerity.

"I know you don't. But you're injured and someone needs to cover your back."

"And that someone is *you*," he said, and the tone of his voice let her know what he thought of that idea.

"I'm better than nothing," she said, and then added, "Don't say I'm not, you know it's true. If these men are as horrible as you say they are, two people are better than one."

"Not when one of them is a pretty woman," he said, "which is why I'm asking you for the last time to turn the truck around and drive to the airport."

She spared him another glance. "I'm relieved to hear you say this is the last time you're asking. It's getting monotonous. Listen, Adam, I promise I'll go meekly away after this little visit. You'll never have to even think of me again."

He opened his mouth to speak and closed it again without uttering a word. What was the point? The woman was impossible.

ECHO PULLED THE TRUCK INTO the Garvey yard.

So, Adam didn't want her here. Tough. He needed someone even if he wouldn't admit it. She'd seen the expression on his face when she touched his shoulder by mistake—thank heavens he was going to the doctor after he dropped her at the airport. Jamie was a nice old guy, but what did he know about medicine?

Anyway, when she'd seen Adam cringe she'd known she couldn't sit at the airport while he came to this house by himself. And she'd been trying all afternoon to keep her distance, to put the day before behind them, to mind her own business and think about her own future. And then that kiss. And then his pain...

She'd found his keys in her pocket and it seemed destiny had forced the issue. Who was she to turn up her nose at fate?

The Garvey house sat halfway between the road and a substantial-looking grove of trees and underbrush to the west. The yard was mostly dirt with patches of stunted grass here and there—in the winter when it rained, it must turn into a giant mud puddle. Two dozen chickens pecked at the ground, weaving their way under and around the dozen or so broken-down cars and trucks. The house itself was a squat bilious cube of yellow asphalt shingles. There were enough abandoned appliances on the sagging porch to start a junkyard.

An old barn with a half-caved-in roof loomed behind the house along with tractors and rusty farm equipment. Echo could see a fenced pasture with scant grass occupied by a dejected-looking brown-and-white cow and three goats.

"Quite the little oasis, isn't it?" Adam said as he undid his seat belt.

"It's pretty desolate."

"Wait here," he said as he opened the passenger door.

She got out of the truck, smiling when he glared at her but he just shook his head in resignation. On the way to the front door, he detoured a few steps and she followed. He gestured at a beat-up old truck with an open trailer hooked to the hitch, an equally battered ATV hunkered in the trailer bed. He walked closer, examining the vehicle before looking over his shoulder at her. "Look familiar?"

"It looks like the one we saw up on the mountain yesterday."

Adam nodded. "I think so, too. If I remind you that he took a shot at you inside the cave, would you reconsider the truck?"

"No."

"I didn't think so."

"He shot at you, too, you know."

"Let's see if anyone's home."

"How many Garveys live here?" she asked as they threaded their way through the flotsam and jetsam of the yard, which included everything from an old suitcase to a box full of pots and pans.

"Willet Garvey and his three remaining sons, two well over twenty and the youngest about sixteen."

"No women?"

"Not presently. I think each boy had a different mother, but there's no one now I know of." He led the way up a couple shallow steps to the porch, dodging split and cracked boards. The screen door squealed as he opened it and knocked.

"I hear a noise inside there," Echo said.

"I do, too."

They waited a few seconds but no one answered. Adam knocked again and called out. "Willet? You in there?"

Echo stepped along the porch. Shading the window with her hand, she tried to see past the smudged, stained glass. It looked like the living room. She could barely discern the edge of a sofa and an overturned lamp.

The rattle of a screen door slamming came from around the house. Startled, Echo jumped. "Adam—"

"He's leaving," he said, and immediately turned to retrace his steps down the stairs. Unfortunately, he landed hard on a rotten board and broke through the wood up to his thigh. He swore as he absorbed the momentum of the fall with his elbows, undoubtedly jarring his injured shoulder yet again.

Echo moved to help him. Her foot caught on another board and it splintered but didn't break. She had to find a spot stable enough to support her weight in order to give Adam a hand. It took forever but at last she got in position and extended a helping hand and he was able to extricate his leg and boot. He limped for a few steps as he continued on around the house.

Echo returned to the front door and tried the knob. It rotated in her hand. Without hesitation, she pushed it open and stepped inside.

The small room was as cluttered as the yard but it was more than that. There'd been a struggle of some kind. The overturned lamp, a card table lying on its side, cards scattered like oversized confetti…

She called out. "Mr. Garvey? Are you in here?"

She spied a shoe in the space between the couch and the kitchen. It took her a second to realize there was a foot inside the shoe and a denim-covered leg above the foot.

She moved quickly. A man lay on the floor, maybe fifty or fifty-five, wiry and gray and unshaven, dressed in jeans and a dirty shirt currently soaked with blood. His face was white though his bare sinewy arms were browned by the sun. One hand lay folded over on itself. The other hand clutched a plastic bag full of white powder.

He was dead. He had to be.

She swallowed revulsion, then she saw his eyelids flicker. Not dead, not yet. She knelt in the narrow space next to him, ignoring something hard beneath her knee.

Twisting her neck, she looked toward the kitchen where she saw the screen door and nothing else.

"Adam?" she called.

Her cell phone was in the truck, buried in her purse. She looked around the room for a telephone but couldn't see one. For the second time in as many days, she wished she had a medical degree.

Was this Willet Garvey? She had no idea though it seemed likely. When his eyelids fluttered again, she offered the only thing she could: soothing words. "Hang on. Adam will be back in a minute. We'll call for help."

His bloody hand pawed at her sleeve, grazed her chest and she gently took it in hers. A spasm shook him. His eyes seemed to focus on her face for a second. "Westin…" he said. His voice was very soft.

She leaned closer. "Please, just relax."

"Tell Den…hat… Westin…"

But that was as much life as he had left. His eyes still half-open, he took a last shuddering breath and lay very still.

Echo released his hand and got to her feet. Something shiny on the floor explained what she'd knelt on—it was an embossed silver disk the size of a fifty-cent piece with two slits cut in the center.

And it looked somehow familiar.

The dead man's last words ran through her mind and suddenly she thought she knew where she'd seen this disk. Her fingers closed over it as a chill clutched at her heart. It couldn't be. *It just couldn't….*

Chapter Seven

By the time Adam had crossed the field and crashed into the underbrush, he was too late; a car raced down the dirt road that bisected the grove and led to the main highway, leaving a billowing cloud of dust in its wake. The haze precluded seeing a license plate let alone getting a number. It was even hard to tell what make or model the car was or what color for that matter.

He'd lost his hat along the way. Wiping a sweaty brow with his good arm, he took a deep breath and turned around.

Had he been chasing one of the Garveys? He didn't think so. To a man, they were all short and lean much like the guy wearing the bandana in the cave the day before. The man he'd pursued, seen only from the back and from a distance, had appeared taller and sturdier.

So why had someone other than a Garvey run away from the house? As he started back across the field, the apprehension he'd been fighting all day was stronger than ever. By the time he whipped his hat off the ground and pulled it back on his head, his gut was telling him that he shouldn't have left Echo alone at that house.

He was in the process of rounding the corner when he heard a sound through the screen door at the rear of the house. He doubled back, stepped up onto the concrete porch and looked through the screen.

Echo must have heard his approach, for the next thing he knew, she appeared at the door, wiping her eyes with a paper towel.

"What in the hell are you doing inside the house?" he demanded, tension making him short. But honestly, trespassing? That's all they needed.

"I saw—"

"Come out of there," he insisted, yanking open the screen door.

"No. You come in."

"I'm not going to compound—"

"Just shut up for a minute and come inside. I think Willet Garvey is lying dead in his living room."

For the first time, he noticed the red stains on her shirt and smears of blood on the towel. "Are you okay?" he asked as he went inside.

He'd never been inside the house and it looked exactly as the outside promised it would look: used, battered, dirty and hopeless. Unfortunately, Echo wasn't mistaken. There was a dead man in the alcove between rooms and it was Willet.

Adam knelt and searched for a pulse though he knew he wouldn't find one. Was this what he'd unconsciously been bracing himself for all day? Not Willet's death specifically, but murder, an escalation in the violence that had been building in the last twenty-four hours?

As he stood, he took in the disarray around him. "It looks as though there was a struggle before he was killed," he murmured as he spotted a shotgun leaning against the wall in the corner.

"Take a look at what's in his hand," Echo said.

His gaze darted to where she pointed. The dead man

clasped a small clear plastic bag sporting a few teaspoons of white powder. Drugs? What else?

"Was he dead when you found him?"

She shook her head. Gesturing at the blood-soaked pillow beside Willet's chest, she said, "I tried—I thought maybe pressure—"

Damn it. He put his arms around her. She came stiffly at first and then more willingly.

"Did he say anything before he died?"

She pulled away, her gaze fastened on Willet's lifeless form. The shake of her head was almost imperceptible.

"Look in the box on the kitchen table," she said, turning away from the dead man.

He went back to the kitchen. A cardboard box that used to hold canned tomatoes sat in the middle of the table, scraps of packing tape cut away so the flaps lay open. Inside the box were several newspaper-wrapped objects. A couple had been partially opened. Adam saw a pottery bowl and what looked like a human skull, an old one judging by the dark brown color.

"Things from your cave?" she asked.

"I think so. Willet must have been the thief."

"If whoever ran away from here killed him, why didn't they take the box?"

"Maybe we interrupted the theft."

She looked perplexed. "Unless that's a bag of sugar in Willet's hand, he's holding something that looks a lot like cocaine. In my business there's a fair amount of it floating around. What's he doing with it? Was he a user?"

Adam shook his head. "I doubt he could afford cocaine. I would think booze would be more…"

At that moment, the front door banged open.

They both whirled around to find a teenage boy standing inside the door. He looked a lot like his brother, Lucas

Garvey, who had worked on the Open Sky Ranch though he wore his sandy hair longer. Same wiry frame and sharp features.

"Are you Dennis?" Adam asked, moving to stop the youngest Garvey before he saw his father.

The boy nodded as he looked from Adam to Echo and back again. "What are *you* doing here? What's going on? Where's my dad?"

Echo moved toward the boy, as well. "Why don't we go outside—"

He ignored her, his gaze fixated on Adam. "I know who you are," he said. "You're one of *them*."

Adam hadn't even been in Wyoming when Dennis's brothers had died, but he knew all the Garveys tended to blame all the Westins for their woes. He needed to get the kid out of the house before things turned ugly.

The boy's gaze went back to Echo. His eyes grew wide as they raked over her, apparently taking in her blood-stained hands and clothes. He looked around the room wildly, then cried out as he tore past Echo and fell to his knees beside his father's still form. He shook the old man's lifeless shoulders. "Dad, Dad…"

"Dennis, come away," Echo said.

"You killed him," Dennis said, his gaze zeroing in on Adam, his voice low and menacing. "You SOB. He knew you were toying with him, he told me that you'd try something. You killed him over some old bones."

The boy was on his feet, fists clenched, face strained. He started to advance on Adam.

Echo caught his arm and he spun around to her, hand raised as though to strike her. "No," she said sternly but with compassion. "He didn't kill your father. I was with him all afternoon and I was here when your father died."

Adam saw something flash behind her eyes as though

an uncomfortable thought had lodged itself in her brain. She all but shook her head as though to get rid it. The boy seemed oblivious to her reaction to her own words, but his hands lowered. Recovering quickly, Echo added, "I'm sorry about your dad. I lost my mother recently. I know how it is."

He stared hard at her a moment, then back down at his father. His gaze went to the bag clutched in the dead fingers.

"Did your father use drugs?" Echo asked.

"No way. Only one used drugs was my brother Doyle and that was a long time ago. Dad beat the tar out of him when he found out." He narrowed his eyes. "Are you saying that bag there is full of some kind of drug? Because if it is, Westin put it there. Dad would never—"

"I don't know what's in the bag," Echo said, "but he was holding it when I found him."

The boy looked around the room as if seeing it for the first time. His gaze extended to the kitchen. By the flicker in his expression, Adam could tell he saw the box on the table and also that he knew exactly what it contained. He looked back at Adam.

"You knew it was Dad. You've been watching him. He told me so."

"No," Adam said, confused. "That's not so. It's true I've been trying to guard the cave because someone has been stealing things, but I didn't know your father was the culprit until today."

"No, you came out here before, he saw you. He told me so."

Adam shook his head.

Echo gently touched the boy's arm. "Let's go outside and call the sheriff. There's nothing for you to do here."

"Yes, there is," Dennis said defiantly and pulled away.

"I gotta find my older brothers. I gotta talk to Hank and Tommy. You ain't gonna get away with this." He patted his pockets as though searching for a cell phone. With one last defiant look at Adam, the boy went outside, the screen door slamming behind him.

"WHAT DO YOU MEAN EVERYONE is gone?" Adam asked Jamie who met him at the end of the driveway to the ranch.

Jamie was at least sixty and had been at Open Sky long before Adam had even been born. Technically, he was the foreman; unofficially, he was one of the family.

He was a bull-legged man, scrappy and opinionated. He had a fond spot for his bay mare and small children and he was one of the few men Adam's father, Birch, ever really listened to.

"We had another tractor breakdown and someone had to go relieve Mike so he could get some sleep. Your dad went after the parts and your brother took off to the cave. Mike got back here about an hour ago looking like something the cat dragged in." Jamie dug in his pocket for a second and hauled out two 9mm bullets. "That reminds me. Mike dug these out of a tree up at the mountain. Said it was near the spent .30 caliber casings Echo shot out of your hunting rifle."

Adam took the bullets. One of them had undoubtedly passed through his shoulder. The invaded skin suddenly throbbed again.

"Me and Pete mowed the rest of the creek field and started in on the north slope. Even Pauline came out and helped for a few hours." The older man rolled his neck and shoulders. Driving a tractor wasn't Jamie's idea of ranching. "Now you tell me a few things. What did the doctor say about you getting shot? I didn't tell your father about it, but I'm not going to start keeping secrets from him at this stage of my life, so you better come clean." Without giving Adam a chance to answer, he added, "Where in the heck have you been all day? Why is Echo still in Wyoming?"

The two men were standing in the middle of the yard. It was almost dark—the day had been unbelievably long, even by ranch standards. Adam looked off toward the house where he knew Echo was telling Pauline and her stepfather all that had transpired that day and knew he needed to do the same. He just wished his father and uncle were here so he only had to go through it once.

"My shoulder is fine," he said. "I didn't make it to the doctor. As for Echo, someone killed Willet Garvey and she happened to be with him when he died so she has to stay around for a while longer."

Jamie whistled. "Willet's dead?"

"Yep. It appears he was our thief. When did Dad leave?"

"Right after you." They both looked up as headlights appeared on the road topping the hillside. Adam hoped it wasn't the police—he and Echo had both spent hours with the sheriff's department that afternoon and had an appointment with him at three the next afternoon for a rehash. When he'd left, deputies had been casting tire tracks out in the grove.

It was his father's old beater that finally swept into the clearing, however. As he got out of the car and pulled on his tan hat, his limp seemed more pronounced than ever.

"Took you long enough," Jamie said.

"No one in Woodwind had it. Good thing Riley's thought to call Big Fir and see if they had one or I'd probably be in Idaho by now. It's in the trunk." He looked at Adam. "You hear about Willet Garvey?"

"Yeah, as a matter of fact—wait, where did you hear about it?"

"On the radio. Can't say it surprises me much."

"Let's go inside and get something to eat," Adam said. "There are things we need to talk about. You come, too, Jamie."

"I already ate. Birch can catch me up on things later." And here he gave Adam a look that telegraphed very clearly that he expected the gunfight of the night before to be disclosed. That data seemed like ancient history to Adam. "Give me your keys, Birch," Jamie added. "I'll go install the part."

"Get Mike to help you," Birch said, tossing the keys to his foreman.

"Mike is sleeping."

"Then Cody—"

"He took his dog with him to guard the cave."

"And Pete?"

Jamie took out the part and a sheet of paper. "Pete worked all day. Now he's inside visiting with Echo I suppose."

"Damn it!" Birch exploded. "This is a ranch in the middle of haying season. What's wrong with everyone?"

"Pauline offered to go after the part for you. You didn't have to run around so stop bellyaching," Jamie sputtered.

"Come inside," Adam said. "We need to talk."

"I don't want to talk. I'll help Jamie—"

"I don't need your help," Jamie said, slamming the trunk. He handed Birch the paper, which appeared to be an invoice. "I'll take an electric lantern out to the field. Now that we have the part, it won't take me more than an hour to fix the tractor. You go inside."

"But—"

"For once, just listen to someone else," Jamie said.

But before anyone could move, more lights showed up on the driveway. Adam steeled himself for another disaster and breathed a sigh of relief when he recognized the long white luxury car that belonged to Lonnie Nielsen.

Lonnie was out of the car in a flash. "I heard about Garvey on the television news," he said. Lonnie wasn't a rancher anymore—he'd lost his place due to some bad investments years ago and now lived on an estate outside Woodwind where his third wife's trust fund kept him comfortable. He was built the same as Adam's father, a big solid man though Lonnie's head was almost completely bald and his eyebrows were all but missing. He wore alligator cowboy boots with red detailing.

"They said you found him," he added, glancing at Adam. He'd stuck his right hand in his jeans pocket and was jingling coins.

"More or less."

"Do they know who did it?"

Birch answered before Adam could. "What are you so steamed up about? I didn't know you and Willet Garvey even knew each other."

"I didn't know him. Never met him," Lonnie said, coins still rattling. "But a murder in broad daylight. It's terrible. No one is safe anymore. Do they know why someone would kill him?"

"Willet had to have a fair number of enemies," Birch said, taking off his hat and scratching his head.

"They said something about a busted drug deal."

"Boy, those newscasters don't miss a beat, do they?" Adam said. "Did they mention the relics, too?"

Lonnie froze. "What relics?" he squeaked at last.

"The relics from our cave," Birch said. "Damn fool was stealing them out of our burial cavern."

"I didn't know you had something like that out here."

"Not many people do. Willet must have heard about it from Lucas or Doyle. Both of them worked here at times. They must have overheard one of us talking about it."

"Was he killed because of those relics?"

"Hell, I don't know," Birch said. He pulled his hat back on his head. "Come on in and have a bite of supper, Lonnie. It's been a long day."

"I can't," Lonnie said, and he turned and opened his car door. "I have to get back to Janine."

Without another word, he squeezed in behind the wheel and started the engine. The tires spun out on the gravel as he whipped the car around and headed back the way he'd come.

Birch shook his head and started up the porch steps. Adam followed, the papers Dr. Wilcox had given him clutched in his hand.

Chapter Eight

Echo looked up from a plate of steaming short ribs she had no appetite for as Birch and Adam came into the house. Her uncle looked grouchy which she was beginning to suspect was a more-or-less chronic condition. Adam looked wired. Her stepfather continued to eat silently.

Adam smiled at her, no doubt noticing her damp hair and change of clothes, maybe even the glass of red wine Pauline had insisted Echo take in the aftermath of her ordeal that afternoon. The truth was the hottest shower and the most potent liquor in the world couldn't chase the image of Willet Garvey's dying face out of her brain.

And his dying words? Her secret. She didn't know what to make of them, she wouldn't repeat them, not to anyone.

And the silver disk? No. There had to be another explanation for that. That would be a secret, too.

The two men sat down at the table as Pauline hurried to bring them cold drinks. Birch dished up a plate for himself and shoved the serving dish toward Adam, who opened an envelope instead, spreading the contents on top of his empty plate.

"What's all that?" Birch asked as he tucked into his dinner.

"These papers are the way we're going to get back to

being ranchers, which is what you keep saying you want. Things have happened you don't know about."

Echo took a deep breath. The atmosphere had suddenly gone from borderline tense to crackling. That plane she hadn't caught looked damn attractive about now.

Didn't it?

It had that morning. Okay, maybe it hadn't in a way. Maybe part of her had wanted to stick around and get to know Adam better. But that kind of stupid thinking was reason enough to get out of here....

"Like what?" Birch said.

Adam pushed himself away from the table. He walked to the unlit dining-room fireplace and rested his good shoulder against the mantle. "Yesterday we were shot at inside the cave. It was a defensive measure used to secure a getaway. Echo fell as a result."

"I know about that—"

"And last night both Echo and I were up on the mountain again. I took a bullet in the shoulder that time. The thief advanced on us when he thought we were down. I wholeheartedly believe we're alive because Echo scared the pants off him."

Pete quietly stared at his stepdaughter.

Echo did her best not to show how pleased Adam's remarks made her. Hopefully he wouldn't mention the fact she had thought she'd killed him....

Birch chewed and swallowed. He accepted a glass of ice water from Pauline and finally said, "Why didn't anyone tell me about this?" Echo noticed how her stepfather avoided Adam's gaze.

"Because I asked them not to. Let me finish. This afternoon I spoke to a professor at the university. They start researching the cave tomorrow morning. They'll handle security until they're done excavating and removing the artifacts to the university for study and proper placement."

Birch took another bite. Echo looked up at Adam and tried to telegraph support—not that he needed it or wanted it from her.

"We've been through this a million times," Birch said at last. "Nothing has changed. Westin men have protected the site since my grandfather's day."

Adam rubbed his eyes. "No, Dad, it's not the same anymore. It used to be a secret of sorts but it's not anymore. Echo and I went out to the Garvey place today. As a matter of fact, she's the one who found Willet. He was still alive, but just barely."

"Still alive!" Birch said, his attention immediately snapping to Echo. The force of his gaze froze her for a second.

"Did he say anything? Did he see who shot him?"

"He didn't speak," she said, and hoped her voice didn't reveal the truth.

Birch rounded on his son. "Why was she the one who found Willet? I can't believe you took her out there. Where the heck were you?"

"I was chasing someone across the field. Someone who left the house right before Willet died. Probably the man who killed him."

"Did you see who it was?" Birch asked anxiously. "Do the police have any suspects?"

"One," Adam said. "Me."

Birch put down his fork. "You!"

"Dennis is convinced I killed his father."

Birch snorted. "Poppycock!"

"I agree. I don't think the sheriff takes it seriously, either. I have an iron-tight alibi because I was with Dr. Wilcox and then with Echo, but that doesn't mean the

Garvey boys won't come looking for revenge. From their point of view, we've pretty much decimated their family and before Willet died, he apparently told his son he'd seen me hanging around their place."

"Was Garvey the scoundrel robbing the cave?"

"It sure looks like it. There's a whole box of artifacts on his kitchen table."

"And now he's dead so that's the end of that," Birch said as he tore a piece of bread and used it to sop up the gravy on his plate.

"No," Adam said firmly, "that's not the end. It's just the beginning."

"Poppycock," Birch repeated.

Pete cleared his throat and spoke for the first time. "Birch is right. If Willet was the thief and now he's dead, no more robberies. What's the point in having the university poking around?"

Adam was working on the knot in his jaw so Echo answered. "The sheriff's office knows those things were taken from your cave. It'll be all over town by tomorrow. Even if Mr. Garvey isn't around to sneak into the cave, someone else will. You'll be stuck posting a guard there until the end of time. Either that, or everything will simply disappear."

She looked from one old man's face to the other, so alike in many ways, especially when it came to stubborn. "And I agree with Adam. There was as much rage in Dennis's face as there was grief. Who knows what he and his brothers will do?"

"We'll just—" Birch began, but Adam turned suddenly and the look on his face was fierce. His father closed his mouth.

"We won't *just* anything," Adam said. "We're going to

invite the university to document and archive that damn burial chamber, to preserve and learn from it. Period."

Birch pushed back his chair and stood. "Are you forgetting who's boss around here?"

"No, sir, I'm not," Adam said. "But your pride is going to get one or more of us killed."

"My pride is what keeps this family going," Birch growled. "My hard work, my—"

"Listen to yourself," Adam said. "Do you really believe you're the only one who's sunk their heart and soul into this place? What about Cody and the price he's paid? What about Jamie and Mike and even me?"

Birch shook his head. "I didn't mean it that way."

"You used to say this was a family ranch. All for one and one for all. I hope you still believe that."

"Of course I do."

"I understand that legally you hold all the power. I'm hoping that your respect and concern for the rest of us is strong enough to open your eyes to this new reality. The whole family is going to be under a microscope until Willet Garvey's murderer is found. Things like this can ruin reputations and lives. It would be great if we could keep the burial cavern intact, the way it was intended, but it's too late for that now. We need to work together and the first order of business is taking care of the past."

"And Cody agrees? Pierce?"

"Both of them. Dad, the dig will be run professionally. Minimal contact with us. They can even use the forest service road on the east side for access. You won't even know it's going on. The remains and artifacts will be photographed in situ and then moved to the university for preservation, just like I said. They'll want to study the cavern, as well, but it won't involve us. And best of all, you will have done the right thing and protected your family in the bargain."

"Just a bunch of academics, huh?"

"That's all. Just a bunch of teachers and students."

"I'll think about it," he said.

Echo took a sip from her wineglass as she looked from father to son. They stood at an angle to her, facing each other. In profile, their appearance was so similar; the male Westin gene pool must be a very strong one. Birch's hair was lighter thanks to the gray and he was a tad shorter in stature and a little heavier, but clothes and hats would mitigate those differences....

Dennis said his father had told him Adam had been watching him, that he'd come out to their house—could Willet have seen Birch, not Adam? Had he seen the concho band and made an assumption he found out today was wrong? Had his dying words not been to indict Adam but to admit he was mistaken?

Equally, was it possible Uncle Birch knew it was Willet behind the thefts? If he had chosen to deal with Willet directly, had he gone there today to reason with him, gotten into a fight—was it possible Birch killed Willet?

What about the drugs? Where did they come in?

"Echo?"

Startled, she set down her glass too quickly and it toppled over, spilling red wine across the white cloth. She gasped, but Pauline simply handed her a napkin.

Adam moved to her side. "You look beat."

She swallowed hard. Where were these crazy thoughts coming from? "Yes, you're right. I am. It's been a terrible day." She gave up on the stain, set the napkin aside and got to her feet. "I'll clear the table—"

"You'll do no such thing," Pauline said. "And Birch, you'd better finish up, sign those papers and get going.

Del Halverson called a while ago to remind you there's a card game tonight over at Lonnie's. He said you should take Pete."

"You guys still playing poker?" Pete asked.

"I missed most the winter 'cause of the leg. Went a couple weeks ago, though. But I doubt Lonnie will have a game tonight. He was here before dinner and seemed real upset. Spooked, even," Birch said.

Adam nodded. "I agree. I think he probably went home and locked all his doors."

"Anyway, we need to see if Jamie got the tractor running. Let's go, Pete."

Echo glanced at the faces around the table. She said a quick good-night and hurried up the stairs to the sanctity of her room.

As ADAM HELPED PAULINE CLEAR the table, he speculated about why Echo had left the table in such a hurry. Of course, watching a man die was bound to upset her.

"Poor kid," Pauline said as she handed him a big bowl to hand dry. "I think you get a little more accustomed to life and death when you live like we do, but she's not used to it."

Did anyone ever get used to violent death? Adam hoped not. As soon as he wasn't needed around the kitchen, he went upstairs where he knocked on Echo's door. She opened it almost at once.

She was barefoot and wore pajamas printed with pink and black rolls of something. He looked closer and realized it was sushi.

"You look good enough to eat," he said jokingly, but it was true and had nothing to do with the pajamas. "May I come in?"

She stood aside. "Of course."

There was a half-empty suitcase on her bed, the one he'd last seen in the back of his truck. "I'm sorry about today," he said.

"You have nothing to be sorry about. It's not your fault I didn't get on that plane."

"I bet now you wish you had." He took a closer look at her face, but she averted her gaze. Was she acting fidgety because she was in nightwear or what is it something else? The pajamas were hardly lingerie.

He took her hand and led her to the flowered upholstered chair by the vanity. "Sit down here for a second. Is there anything I can get you? Tea, something stronger—"

"Nothing," she said.

He sat opposite her, resting on the edge of the bed. For a second, they stared at each other and then she looked down at her hands. "Did you want something specific?" she asked. "Is something on your mind?"

The truth was a simple: *You. You're on my mind.* Instead, he said, "Well, first of all, I'm sorry you were alone when Willet died. I should have stayed. If there'd been another killer, you might have been hurt."

"But I wasn't," she said.

"You had to watch a man die. *That's* hurt."

She nodded, her eyes wide and dark as she glanced up at him. "Yes. I won't forget that."

"And second of all, I want to apologize for bringing up the university thing at the dinner table. I knew it was going to make a lot of sparks. I should have waited."

She looked at him funny. "It's okay, Adam. This is important and besides, this is your family, not mine."

He stood up and came to stand in front of her. She met his gaze quickly, then peered down at her lap again.

He caught her hands in his and pulled her to her feet. "Don't say that. This is your family, too."

"Not the same way it is yours."

"I don't know what you mean."

She shook her head as though unwilling to elaborate, disengaged her hands and sidled past him. On the way toward the window, she paused to look at the grouping of framed photographs on the wall.

"That's Cody's wedding picture," Adam said, gesturing at the photo of Cody and the blonde bride beside him.

"Her name is Cassie, right?"

"Yes," he said, coming up behind her to look at the picture. He hadn't seen it in a long time.

"She's very pretty."

"You'd like her."

Echo hugged herself and looked around the room. "I feel like I know her. It's like she's a ghost in this house. Her and your mother, both."

He knew what she meant. He'd felt it himself.

She turned suddenly, catching her breath when she realized how close he stood.

Her brow creased. "Doesn't it strike you as odd that my stepfather sold his share of the ranch and moved us away after your mother left? That meant your father was stuck here with three small boys and a huge ranch to manage on his own."

"Well, there was Pauline and Jamie—"

Her glance this time was longer, her brow still furrowed. "And what about vacations? Why didn't you guys ever come to Frisco? Why didn't we ever come back here? Over twenty years, even when my mother was ill, nothing except a few letters and email, an occasional picture. Why?"

"I don't know why. No one ever asked me and I never gave it much thought. Now, of course, I wish I had." He raised a hand and stroked her cheek, pleased when her eyelids flickered at his touch.

"What do you mean?" she whispered.

"You know what I mean."

"No—"

"Why didn't you leave today?"

"I told you—"

"Was it because of the way I kissed you?"

"You were just trying to annoy me."

"Partly," he admitted. "It may have started out that way but by the end, things had changed. Is that why you stayed?"

"You were hurt—"

"Be honest."

"What do you want me to say? That I'm attracted to you? That you're sexy as all get-out and I've entertained decidedly un-cousin-like thoughts about you?"

"Yes and yes and yes," he said, smiling, but a second later, when her petal soft lips brushed his, the smile faded away.

He let himself go, his tongue running along her lips, tasting every nuance. He'd known her as an adult for a whopping thirty-six hours. They'd shared a dozen kisses and each one seemed to inch them along a quivering thread toward some conclusion he couldn't foresee. He didn't want to look too far ahead; he wanted to stay in the moment. He pressed her closer.

And she came. For once there was no pulling away by either of them. Adam wasn't sure what fueled her response, wasn't sure he wanted to know. She'd been edgy when he first came to her room, fidgety and distracted, but now she was like wax set close to a flame, soft and incredibly accessible. She awoke parts of him that he'd never dreamed she could touch.

He ran his hands down her back, aching to strip away her pajamas and gaze at the wonders that were so close. Her bottom was firm, the luscious feel of her ripe breasts pressed against his chest set him on fire. Every male part of him was ready to leap tall buildings if that's what it took to bury itself in her.

"Echo," he whispered into her hair and even her name sounded different on his lips. He sucked her tender earlobe as his hand traveled up under her pajama top. Her skin was velvet and satin but best of all, his touch sent a discernible shiver through her supple body. She drew away an inch and grasped his shoulder. Her fingers grazed the gunshot wound but he didn't care.

"This is too fast," she said.

"No, it's been coming."

"You don't know me."

"I know you."

"I was married before. Did you know that?"

"No," he said, kissing her throat as he unbuttoned her top. "And I don't care."

"Oh, what's happening?" she murmured. Her eyes were half-closed, dark and mysterious; cheeks flushed, lips moist and full.

"We're both finally being honest at the same time," he said, nuzzling her neck as a second button slipped undone.

"That's what this is—honesty?"

"Honesty wrapped in lust. I want you. I have since the moment I laid eyes on the grown-up you. I'm tired of fighting it."

"You should go…."

"Come with me," he interrupted. All the obstacles that had seemed so important just that morning now seemed insignificant. The third button slid open and his breath caught at the sight of her breasts. Perfect. He dipped his head to lick her left nipple. "Don't say no," he whispered.

"I should go to bed."

He raised his head and stared into her eyes. "Yeah. With me."

Her lips parting caused a sensation that went straight to his groin.

"Meet me outside in ten minutes," he added, his voice deeper than usual. Without giving her a chance to refuse, he kissed her one last time and left the room.

Chapter Nine

Echo threw on jeans and a light sweater. She left off underwear. What was she thinking? This was nuts!

She was tired of thinking. That's what she was thinking.

The house seemed deserted as she flew down the stairs and let herself out the front door. She expected to find Adam sitting in his truck, waiting for her.

Instead, she saw him astride Solar Flare, man and horse perfectly positioned to catch the full strength of the moonlight. Her breath caught in her throat. Suddenly shy, she approached slowly.

He rode bareback.

He lowered his hand and she took it. With an impressive show of strength, he pulled her up behind him where she circled his waist with her arms and leaned her cheek against his back.

They hadn't spoken a word and their silence continued as Adam guided the horse down the slope and around the pond. It didn't take Echo very long to figure out they were headed to his house, and she smiled as she had recalled telling him that he'd reminded her of a Bowerbird building an elaborate nest to attract a mate. Was that because he didn't think he alone was enough for a woman?

Too much thinking. Turn off the brain.

Listen to the sound of hooves, feel the heat of the man in front of you, breathe deeply of mountain air tinged with the latent smell of freshly cut hay. Make a memory to take along for the rest of your life.

The lake soon appeared, dappled with moonlight, still and lovely. Adam's dark house towered on the point near the grove of trees.

He stopped the horse way before the house, and lowered her to the ground. She landed softly on the grass. A second later he was beside her. He patted Solar Flare's butt. The horse whinnied softly before ambling off to graze nearby.

And then she was in Adam's arms again and this time she knew there was no going back.

He pulled her sweater over her head almost at once. When he saw she wasn't wearing a bra, his gaze landed on hers and the moonlight revealed a smile on his lips. She pulled off his shirt carefully and ran her fingers across the sculpted muscles that hard work had defined in his chest.

"Does it hurt?" she whispered, touching his skin near the bandaged flesh.

"No," he murmured, and sitting, tugged her to the grass beside him. Slowly, deliberately, they peeled away socks and boots and jeans. It was just the two of them, naked flesh shimmering in the moonlight as they fell onto each other.

She wasn't a virgin. She'd been taking birth control for years, but for some reason, she'd never made love outdoors before, and never with a man who looked like a god in the moonlight or one who knew exactly where to touch her to send her screaming blindly into the night.

His mouth was all over her, warm and delicious, turning her inside out. She followed suit, covering him with kisses, his erection between them, hard as steel, potent and exciting. She wasn't sure how he held off but he did, sending her into a spate of orgasms with his mouth and fingers that left her too weak to move. But he coaxed her back to life, his touch delicate yet firm. When he came inside her, the power of his thrusts rocked her off her axis. And when he exploded, she laughed and sobbed simultaneously deep inside her gut from the sheer impact of emotions clashing together like cross currents of a raging river.

And he was still there. His fingers rubbed her nipples, caressed her bottom, stroked her thighs.

"Do you like the water?" he whispered into her ear.

"Yes."

"Come with me," he said, and rising, pulled her to her feet. The way his gaze traveled up and down her nude body sent more heat waves flashing through her core as he led her to the lake's edge.

The water was warm and silky, the bottom of the lake smooth and easy to walk on. Holding hands, they waded in until only their heads were above the water.

"Come here," he said, pulling her into an aquatic embrace. The feel of his wet body rubbing against hers sent more sparks shooting into the sky.

Eventually, she lay on her back floating, her extended hand resting in his as he floated beside her. *How did we get to this point after the day we had?* she wondered, staring up at the moon. To him she said, "I wish this night could last forever."

"Me, too," he whispered.

More silence, easy and comfortable. Then, "Echo? What happened to your marriage?"

She'd known he'd come back to that eventually. She

waited a few seconds to respond, wondering how honest to be. Might as well go for the gold.

"The surface facts are simple. Married senior year of college, him idealistic and earnest, me dumb as a post."

He chuckled softly. "A lot of marriages start like that. So what happened?"

"He wasn't what I thought he was. Truthfully, I don't think he was what he thought he was, either."

"And all that means—"

"As long as there are young men telling themselves lies, there will be young women buying into them. He thought he wanted to save the world. What he really wanted was to see how many women he could get into bed."

"Was he good at it?"

She smiled. "Are you asking if he was good getting a woman into bed or good once he was there?"

"I'm not sure," he said, his thumb running across her wet palm.

"It doesn't matter. He was adequate in both departments. I left when it all became too much."

"You make it sound as though his infidelity didn't matter to you."

"Do I?" she said softly. "If I do, it's an act. It was terrible. It ate away at my self-worth until I just got sick of it—and him. And if I sound callous, that's because several years have passed and it seems like it all happened to someone else now."

"I'd like to kick him in the teeth."

She smiled up at the stars. "My hero."

He righted himself and grabbed her. "Are you making fun of me?"

"Absolutely not," she said immediately before his lips landed on hers again.

But this time he was the one who cut things short. "I should have relieved Cody an hour ago up at the cave."

The mention of the cave was like an alarm ringing during a wonderful dream; reality crashed around her. She stopped floating and found they'd drifted away from shore. They swam back slowly, emerging from the water reluctantly. Solar Flare was only a few feet away, staring at them.

It didn't take long for the warm air to dry them sufficiently to pull their clothes back on and remount the horse. Echo fell silent as increasingly distraught thoughts raced through her mind. How could she have allowed herself this last hour when she had harbored such terrible suspicions about Adam's father? Even though she hadn't said a single word about her doubts, it felt to her like she'd lied. Would Adam have wanted her the way he had if she had told him what she had suspected?

After dinner she'd checked out a photo stored in a file on her laptop, the one of Adam's graduation. As she'd recalled, it was a father-and-son snapshot, both men in Stetsons, Uncle Birch's black with a distinctive concho headband.

And the silver disk she'd taken from the Garvey house matched the three on the hat perfectly. She'd known the moment she had found it that it was going to be a match. She just didn't know what it meant and she wasn't sure who to ask to find out. The truth was she hadn't seen Uncle Birch wear that hat since she had arrived here.

She had to talk to Adam. She'd just made love to him, for heaven's sake. Surely she could trust him to help her figure out what she was missing, why she was wrong.

"Did your father sign the papers?" she said, hoping it was a good place to begin.

"I'm not sure. I'll check when I get to the house."

She kissed his neck and tightened her arms around his solid torso as they rode Solar Flare. "Did he find the part he went after?"

"For the tractor? Yeah. He had to drive to Big Fir."

"Hmm— How long does it take to drive to Big Fir?"

"From here?"

"From Woodwind."

"Less than an hour."

"And he left here at noon."

Adam's back stiffened a bit. "He had trouble finding the part, he had to go from store to store."

"How many stores in Woodwind?"

"That carry this kind of equipment? One, maybe two. What are you driving at?"

"Nothing," she said, afraid to push further.

"Something is on your mind," he said. "Spit it out."

"No, I'm not ready."

He turned to glance at her over his shoulder. "Echo, it's me you're talking to. I know something is wrong. I felt it when I came into your room. In fact, before that, down at dinner. Then I got distracted. What is it?"

She bit her lip as she drank in his handsome face. Wait a second. Since when was she afraid to speak her mind? "Well, do the math. Forty minutes into Woodwind from here. Two hours driving around town looking for the part. That's a generous three hours. That means he exhausted his search in Woodwind before three o'clock, probably well before. Why did it take him almost another five hours to drive less than an hour and buy a part?"

He had turned away from her to guide the horse, but his silence was absolutely deafening.

She pulled away again. "Never mind. This has been eating away at me all evening but now that I'm saying it out loud, I wish I could take it back. I mean, maybe he stopped for a snack or maybe he had to search through several stores once he got to Big Fir."

Adam shook his head, releasing a few drops of water that landed on her face. "He didn't have to search when he got to Big Fir," he said at last. "The store in Woodwind called ahead. The part was waiting for him."

"Oh."

"You found Willet at three-thirty?"

"I looked at my watch when he died. It was 3:25."

He turned for a quick look. "Are you saying I chased my own father through the field? Are you accusing him of killing Willet?"

"I don't know, Adam. But he did return tonight with a worse limp than he had this morning. And you and he do sort of look alike, especially from a distance. It would be possible to confuse you. And Dennis said his father suspected you were onto him. Maybe it was your father Willet saw and just thought it was you."

She couldn't bring herself to repeat Willet's dying words or mention the concho she'd plucked off the floor. But it was in the Garvey house and unless there was a duplicate, didn't it suggest a Westin had been inside the house, too, probably Birch? Gently, she said, "Maybe your father just came to talk and found Willet already dying."

"And ran off and left him without helping? That's even worse. Anyway, Dad would have taken the artifacts with him."

Their voices dropped to whispers as though the night had ears. "Maybe he planned to but then heard us at the door and panicked."

They had reached the house. He got off first this time and reached up to help her down. She wished she could stay within the circle of his arms where she landed.

"The invoice," he said.

"What invoice?"

"From the store. They stamp the time of transaction on those things. If we can find it, we can check it out."

The house was dark but the door was unlocked. They crossed the hall to the den the ranch used as its business office. Adam flicked on the light as they entered and Echo closed the door softly behind them.

She hadn't been in the office in over twenty years but it looked exactly as she had remembered it. Same leather furniture, big fireplace, gun cabinet. An oil painting of an old house that looked vaguely familiar hung behind the desk and a tray holding a couple liquor bottles and crystal glasses sat near a large window, the drapes drawn for the night. The only clue that time had advanced was the computer and printer on a corner table.

"Would you pour me a whiskey?" he asked. "Help yourself to whatever you'd like."

She poured whiskey in two glasses and handed him one. He'd moved behind the desk and sat in the swivel chair. The papers before him appeared to be the university forms.

"Did he sign them?" she asked as she moved behind him. He smelled like the lake, fresh and summery, and she wanted to kiss his head. She didn't.

"Yeah, he did. I half expected he wouldn't."

She had, too.

He plucked a yellow paper from atop a shallow stack and checked the letterhead. "This is the invoice." He placed it on the desk directly under the lamp. Echo moved to look closer.

The printer that had created the invoice obviously needed a new ink cartridge. As a result, data was hard to decipher. Echo crossed mental fingers that if they ever spotted a time of transaction it would reveal Birch Westin had been in Big Fir buying a tractor part when Willet Garvey heaved his last breath.

"There's the date," she said, pointing at numbers in an upper right box.

He tilted the paper toward himself and studied it a second. "The time is underneath it. Five fifty-five p.m."

"That leaves a couple hours unaccounted for," she whispered.

"There has to be another explanation," Adam said.

"Of course," she said, ignoring her drink. The uncertainty she'd managed to instill in Adam's voice made her queasy. She moved around where she could see his face and perching on her heels, took his hands in hers. "Talk to your father. He'll tell you—"

"He'll tell me nothing. When he gets wind I'm questioning his character, he'll throw me off this ranch. And I won't blame him."

"Adam—"

"What about the drugs? How do you explain those?"

She released his hands and stood up. "I don't. That's where this falls apart." *Tell him about the concho....*

He stared at her a second or two, downed the rest of his drink with a single swallow and set the glass carefully and deliberately on the desk. He took a deep breath. "No, that's not where it falls apart. It fell apart when I began to buy into your crazy theory. Damn."

He straightened the university forms and placed the invoice back on the right stack of papers, his movements exact. Her heart felt ponderous in her chest. "Adam? Please, talk to me."

"I don't know if I should right now."

"You're upset...."

"Damn right I'm upset. It obviously didn't occur to you to take into consideration some pretty intangible factors."

"Such as?"

"Honesty. Integrity."

Sympathy and guilt flew straight out the window in light of his holier-than-thou stance. "Oh, that's right," she said, striding away from him. "Those are qualities every Westin male embraces with every waking breath. How could someone like me ever hope to understand such decency?"

"I guess you can't."

She rounded abruptly and glared at him. "*You* asked *me* to confide in you."

"How was I supposed to know you were entertaining the notion that my father is capable of cold-blooded murder? It's insane."

"All I'm asking is you keep an open mind," she said softly. Despite her frustration with him, the storm raging in his gray eyes made her cringe. How she wished she'd kept these suspicions to herself until she had proof. If she ever had proof. She would ask her uncle about the hat. She would not involve Adam again....

"Cody's waiting for me to relieve him at the cave," he said, avoiding her gaze.

"Adam, please. I'm not accusing your dad of a thing. It's all speculation."

He stared straight into her eyes. "You know, Echo? That somehow makes it worse." He walked to the door and opened it. Holding it wide, he gestured with his good arm. "After you."

Chapter Ten

The campfire Cody had built outside the cave acted as a beacon, but Adam thought it would also warn anyone intent on mischief that the cave was guarded.

As he drew close, he could see Cody stretched out on the ground leaning against a rock. A tin pot sat nearby on a different rock, this one with a distinct slant. Bonnie stood near the edge of the firelight, tail wagging. Adam knew she would have barked had she not recognized his scent.

He tied Solar Flare to a tree and patted the dog.

"You look like you're settled in for the night," he said as he approached.

Cody yawned. "Ground's a little hard. You here to spell me?"

Adam found a spare mug in the supplies and poured himself a cup of cowboy coffee from the tin pan. The slant of the settling brew had gathered the grounds on one side of the pan, but it was still tricky getting something he could drink. After the whiskey, though, he needed a pick-me-up.

After the whiskey and Echo.

"Where's your sidekick?" Cody asked as he felt around for his hat.

Adam cast his brother a glowering look. "What side-kick?"

A rare grin played around with the corners of Cody's mouth. "The pretty one. Seems you two have been hanging out together a lot. You know, sharing adventures and things. Is there something going on you want to tell your big brother?"

Cody could have no idea how his joke cut through Adam's heart. He'd had everything he wanted an hour ago. "Not a thing," he growled.

"You sure? She's got a way about her. Seems to me she might have her sights set on you."

"Listen, if you're so anxious to sit here and gossip, why don't you admit why you really called Pierce home while I was in Hawaii? Why you really ran off into the dead of night? That detective you hired found Cassie, didn't he? That's why you left. Did you finally talk to her?"

All hint of amusement slid from Cody's lips. "How do you know about the detective?"

"I live here. I know."

Cody shook his head. "Leave it alone."

"Well, did you see her? Did you have it out? Is it over for good now? Can you get on with things?"

"It wasn't her," Cody said, his voice barely a whisper. "It isn't over."

Feeling lower than a rattlesnake, Adam mumbled, "Sorry I asked."

They fell into an uneasy silence until Cody took a deep breath and started to rise. "Anyway, I forgot you dropped off Echo at the airport. She's back in California by now."

"Can we just not talk about Echo? There's a whole lot that went on today you don't know about. Sit a minute while I fill you in."

He gave Cody the abbreviated version of the afternoon,

hitting the major high spots and completely leaving out any mention of Echo's absurd observations let alone the hour of passion they'd shared before she'd made them. After they mulled over the facts a little, Adam brought up the other thing that was worrying him.

"I can't stop thinking about the way the gunman charged up the hill after us last night. Seems out of character for Willet."

Cody tossed the cold dregs of his cup into the bushes. "I've been thinking about that since you mentioned it earlier so when I got here tonight, I took a tour of the cave. I got to thinking that maybe what could have caused him to get brave all of a sudden was if he was ready to haul everything away. But it doesn't look like anything inside the cave has changed since you ran someone out of there yesterday. The lock hasn't been tampered with, nothing."

The brothers stared into the flames for a minute, then Cody got to his feet. "Come on, Bonnie, time for you and me to head home for some shut-eye."

After he left, Adam stoked the fire and prayed something would happen at the cave to divert his attention. Nothing happened. *Nothing.*

His thoughts circled around Echo like vultures around a dead carcass. He knew he should never think about her again but he couldn't stop. She'd been such a huge part of the events of the past two days. Front and center you could say. Hell, he almost expected her to materialize even now. She wouldn't be welcome but when did that ever stop her?

He peered into the shadows.

He'd never made love to a woman like her before. She'd consumed him, brought out things in him he didn't even know about himself. His brain told him to stay clear of her while every other part of his body urged him to sell his pride down the creek and go back to her.

Why did she have to come here, anyway? She was dangerous—he'd known it from the minute he had spied her long ivory legs, but he'd allowed her sexy, sassy beauty to trick his hormones into thinking she was worth a little trouble.

Life was a game to her. People were pieces to be shuffled around a board. Or a television show...

And yet, damn it, some of what she had said made sense. He'd had hazy questions about his father's motives, too. None as outlandish as hers and none he'd ever give voice to. Allowing her to say those things about his dad while seated in what they all thought of as *his* office had made Adam feel like Benedict Arnold. And worse, way worse, *he'd* bought into them for a minute.

A ranch ran on trust and guts and believing the best of those you depended on for your livelihood and sometimes for your very life.

But what *had* taken the old man so long? And why hadn't he taken Pauline up on her offer to fetch a part—she was used to being the gofer. Birch had work to do, things at the ranch he was anxious about, so why squander all that time?

Mike relieved Adam at daybreak. A quick ride home, an even quicker shower, then out in the field, manning a tractor, making patterns in the tall grain fields, wishing the gulped breakfast Pauline had forced him into eating wasn't sitting like a pile of rusty horseshoes in his gut.

Dr. Wilcox showed up late and from the wrong direction. She'd obviously been to the house first. He'd been making big passes across the field and had apparently missed her van the first time she went by.

He stopped the tractor and walked over to the road

where she'd pulled to the side and rolled down the window. "I hate to bother you, but I need to see the forms," she told him.

"That's okay. I have them right here." As he took them out of his vest pocket, he glanced inside the big van—it was empty except for Wilcox and one passenger, a man in his late forties with a high forehead and sparkling eyes. He wore jeans and a cotton jacket. A watch that appeared to tell the time at any given spot in the world looked heavy on his wrist.

"This is Professor Lavel, the visiting archaeologist I was telling you about," Wilcox said as Adam handed her the signed papers.

"Call me *Henri*," Lavel said with a French accent, leaning over Dr. Wilcox to offer his hand in greeting. "*Monsieur,* how I look forward to this cave of yours!"

"That's good to know," Adam said, shaking Lavel's hand.

Wilcox opened the papers and scanned for the signatures. "The students are checking our equipment back at your place," she said. "Your housekeeper said there's a man out there already who can show us around."

"Yeah, Mike's there. But you'll need a guide to find it in the first place. Give me a minute to alert the others and move the tractor—"

"No, no, I grew up on a farm, I know about harvesting schedules," she said. "We won't disrupt you."

"But after all, there is no need," Lavel gushed, rubbing his hands together in anticipation. "Your lovely cousin has volunteered to show us to the cave. I gather she is looking forward to the *expédition.*"

His *cousin.* Adam looked down at the ground. Echo showing them the way to the cave rankled every bone in his body and yet there was no denying she was competent to do it; she'd found her way there alone night before last, and after dark to boot. It was just that everywhere she went something awful seemed to happen and it made him uneasy.

He looked out over the waving acres of grass that needed to get mowed. He glanced back at the two expectant professors.

Wilcox smiled, her teeth as white as the high clouds floating overhead. "Don't worry, Mr. Westin. We know our way around a cave. You do your thing and let us do ours and we'll meet back at your house at four this afternoon to see what we have."

"We will take excellent care of your cousin. You need have no fears," Lavel added.

He wished people would stop calling Echo his cousin. Maybe the label had fit as good as any other at one time but it no longer sat comfortably. Way too much had passed between them. For a moment there, she'd been his lover....

Let it go.

Right now the question was, did he warn them not to take anything Echo said too literally? Like maybe Birch Westin had motive and means to kill a man.

No. Whatever Echo was, she wasn't thoughtlessly cruel.

"Just do me a favor and remind her that she's due back here by three for a chat with Sheriff Inkwell."

ECHO DROVE A RANCH ATV IN the lead of the other five vehicles that carried the professors, three graduate students and a lot of supplies. They had to pass the big house by the lake to get to the trail leading to the caves and she avoided glancing at it.

As for the lake itself—it lay there in the sunshine, blue, inviting and heartbreaking.

Mike, whom she hadn't yet met, turned out to be a

large affable guy with short curly black hair and biceps the size of Easter hams. He cheerfully greeted everyone and unlocked the cave, then walked ahead down the rock-strewn descent with a flashlight as Echo lit the torches the way Adam had the time before. She barely paused at the spot where she'd first kissed him, hoping to rattle him a little.

The main cavern was exactly as it had been the only other time she'd been there, the stalagmites making for tricky walking, the sound of dripping water in the background, the growing chill as they descended farther into the earth. The pickax still lay on the ground where the thief had dropped it while dark shadows on the far side hid the shaft into which she'd fallen when the thief had shot at her.

Had it been Willet Garvey?

Mike stepped forward and lowered his voice. "I've never been in here before. Do you know the way to the burial cavern?"

"I saw Adam go down this tunnel," she said, lighting yet another torch.

Both professors and the student archaeologists alike had been taking numerous photos as they moved through the cave, each step accompanied by the metallic jingle of equipment. Lavel sometimes broke into rapid-fire French in his excitement. He came forward to walk with Echo, holding her elbow as he asked a million questions she couldn't answer.

The narrow secondary tunnel eventually stopped by a pile of rocks. Evidence of a wood door lay shattered on the ground, thanks, no doubt, to the pickax left back in the main cavern. It crossed Echo's mind to ask around and see if anyone had thought to check the handle of the ax for prints, although a man using such a tool generally wore gloves.

Wilcox held an arm out at her side to stop everyone from entering. "Allow Professor Lavel to go first," she said.

"*Madame,* that honor should go to you. This is your dig," Lavel said gallantly.

"Please, be my guest."

Niceties out of the way, Lavel stepped into the cavern. He carried a very powerful flashlight, which he used to illuminate the walls and floor and the ceiling overhead. Wilcox and the students crowded close behind him, filling the entrance, shining their lights, as well. As a result, the small chamber burst into light.

It was a space of high walls and many fissures of varying lengths and widths. A huge pile of rocks occupied much of the center space, one shaped more or less like a big stone chair or throne. What appeared to be a deep rift in the floor two-thirds of the way into the room looked menacing. A metal cart filled with several wrapped bundles that resembled those Echo had seen in the box on top of Willet Garvey's kitchen table sat off to one side.

Should she tell Wilcox and Lavel about those items? No doubt they were in police custody by now; she'd leave that disclosure to Adam. But she did remember part of the conversation from two days before and repeated it now, Adam's voice ringing in her ears just as it had the first days before. "I'm told the native tribe who summered in this high valley used this cavern to bury their dead. Adam said they wrapped the body, and sometimes personal items, in blankets."

Dr. Wilcox murmured assent. "It was a common practice. I've been in mortuary caves before, but none this far west."

"This cave is a little modern for me," Lavel said, as he bent down to examine something on the rocky floor. "The last excavation I led went back three thousand years. It is a shame, no, that there has been so much tampering? Still, this will be most interesting. Most interesting." He got to his feet and approached the large rift in the floor. Looking over his shoulder, he called, "Dr. Wilcox, we must descend this crevasse and photograph what lies at the bottom. Everyone come in now, but be careful where you step, there are pieces of remains strewn about."

Dr. Wilcox began issuing directions and Echo did her best to stay out of the way. It was cold this deep underground and creepy despite the fact the torches had been lit in the cavern. There was talk of bringing in a generator so they wouldn't add to the damage by continuing to use the kerosene torches.

She didn't think of the people buried here as ghosts, but there was a definite feel to the place. A musty, dank odor permeated her nostrils. Sounds were muffled as everyone worked with practiced discipline. Echo knew this was a survey-and-assessment phase and she was impressed with the professionalism of the procedure.

After an hour, she found a rock that no one seemed interested in and sat down. Nearby, Wilcox and Lavel discussed how they would construct a grid the next day and made equipment lists. The students had rigged a halter and one had descended into the large chasm. The continual snapping and flashing of cameras was ever present.

Mike sidled up to her. She wasn't sure where he'd been, had all but forgotten about him. "Think it's all right if I leave?" he asked her.

"Sure."

"What about locking it when they're done?"

"I heard two of the students say they were spending

the night outside the entrance. I don't think you're going to have to come out here anymore."

"That's okay with me. Kind of gives me the willies. Hate to leave you here alone, but I'm supposed to ride the summer pasture today. We delivered the bulls up there a couple weeks ago."

"The bulls?"

Mike winked. "Now you know where next year's calves come from."

She laughed with him. "Ah…"

"Plus occasionally a coyote goes after one of the calves and I need to—"

"Mike, I'm okay here. Go back to work."

"If you're sure."

"Positive. But on your way out, will you set the pickax aside so no one touches it? There may be prints. Use a cloth or something."

He shook his curly head. "Sorry, Miss, guess I goofed. I picked it up a few minutes ago when I cleared the path. I didn't think about prints."

She plastered on a smile. "It was a long shot. Don't worry about it."

He loped off on his giant feet and she contemplated leaving, too. It wasn't like she was actually helping.

On the other hand, she was safe from Adam inside this cave. Every detail of the night before was so clear it hurt. Every kiss, every whispered word, every touch. Each one had an identity, each one played and replayed in her brain. She was near tears one moment, furious with him the next, anxious to see him and find out if a night's rest had changed the way they had left things, just as anxious to never see him again.

What if he dismissed her the way he had last night? Self-protection kept her backside glued to the rock.

The sound of voices roused her from a stupor some time later and she stood and stretched, surprised two hours had passed. Thanks to Adam, she hadn't slept well the night before and she smothered a yawn with her fist.

The student who had been lowered into the chasm was pulled free a few minutes later. "The main platform is thirty-three-point-five meters down and six meters long," he reported. "It drops off in a narrower chasm at the far end. The light picked up traces of remains and debris down there, too. Here, I took photos of the main ledge."

He handed the digital camera to Wilcox and she and Lavel scrolled through the shots on the view screen, Lavel exclaiming with delight when he caught a glimpse of something interesting. Echo was curious what the chasm looked like but shy about barging in so she stayed back, but it soon became clear something in the atmosphere had changed.

She looked at Lavel's face and found his eyebrows squeezed together as Wilcox held and operated the camera. "Go back one, no another," Lavel said, his accent thicker than before but his voice hushed. "*Oui, Madame,* there. Go ahead now, see if he got closer. Rogers? Join us, *s'il vous plaît.*"

The students had long since stopped talking and stood as a unit nearby. Rogers, the man who had taken the pictures, stepped over to the camera and the conversation grew softer.

"What is it? What's wrong?" Echo asked.

Wilcox looked up from the small screen. "We're not sure what we're looking at. We'll need to take another peek, that's all. Part and parcel of the work. Why don't you go back to the ranch, Miss De Gris? Your cousin said I was to mention you have an appointment with the sheriff at three. There's nothing you can do here and sooner or later we'll need you out of this cavern so we can conclude our assessment."

Echo studied the professor's face and felt one-hundred-percent certain she was hiding something. She stepped closer. "Is there something down in the chasm?"

"Remains and artifacts alike," Lavel said impatiently. He had stepped into the harness and was buckling the straps. "And someone put the garbage. *Imbeciles!*"

"Garbage? Like what?"

"Wrappers, the aluminum cans."

"Those things might be important," Echo said excitedly. "They might have fingerprints on them. They could help the police identify the man who disturbed this spot." She didn't add that they might also tie into a murder. "It's important you recover them with care," she continued. "I produced a show on police procedure when I was an intern during college. Wear gloves and put things in paper sacks or better yet leave them in place—"

Lavel interrupted her with an impatient twist of his hand. "Miss De Gris, we know how to process all sorts of evidence, both of the past and the present. We do not, how you say, *manhandle* objects of any nature. Please, do not worry."

His charm had certainly slipped a notch or two.

Dr. Wilcox smiled nervously as though anxious to smooth ruffled feathers.

Echo backed down, thinking clearly at last. What if something down there revealed Birch Westin had been out here with Willet Garvey? Maybe Birch had been more involved than even she suspected. Maybe that's why he was dragging his feet about allowing the dig. Merciful heavens, what if he'd been in cahoots with Garvey?

And what if she had now made sure that possible evidence of that meeting would be saved and processed?

She said her goodbyes hastily, anxious not only for fresh air but to find Adam and prepare him if she could.

She just wasn't sure what she was preparing him for—or if he would listen to her.

Chapter Eleven

Sheriff Clayton Inkwell was a man whose appearance misled the unwary. It wasn't just the mass of white-blond bristly hair that escaped his cap, or the unshaven chin or even the dusty green uniform. It was something in his eyes, lurking there in the pale blue depths, that hinted you could tell him whatever you wanted. Heck, he was just putting in time until he retired in a couple years; he was a good old boy and about as smart as a grasshopper.

Adam knew none of it was true. He suspected Inkwell would be reelected as Woodwind's sheriff until he sat down at his desk one day and keeled over dead. And he would be reelected because of one reason: come hell or high water, he got things done.

Why was Echo late for this meeting? He knew she was back. He'd caught sight of her a few times in the field but he'd gone out of his way to avoid her. Once that meant turning the tractor and going back over land that had already been mowed which was a giant waste of time but he didn't care. As far as he was concerned, they had nothing left to say to one another.

Unless she'd somehow managed to single-handedly blow up the cave and the whole team of archaeologists inside it and he doubted that.

He and the sheriff sat on a bench in the shade. Pauline

delivered iced tea and they chatted about the last time Inkwell had been at the house, right after Pierce and Princess Analise's problems. Adam wanted the sheriff busy elsewhere before Wilcox and the others returned. The cave thing had to go smoothly or his father might well rescind permission. Thinking about his father didn't help Adam stay calm.

He used to be the even-keeled one. Pierce was the rebel. Cody was the tip-of-the-iceberg type. They all had their roles. His was Mr. Take-It-Easy.

But you wouldn't know it now, not since Echo had showed up.

"Why don't I just go over my story again," he finally said. "Echo and you can mosey inside and talk about her part when she decides to show up."

Inkwell crossed his arms over his chest. "Oh, that's okay. I got me nowhere else more important to be and I'd rather do it this way. Don't like chewing the fat twice." He paused a second and nodded toward the fields. "Anyway, she's coming right now," he added.

Adam turned to find a horse at full gallop covering the newly mown field. "I doubt that's her."

But he was wrong, it was Echo. She was on the big bay gelding and she handled him now as though she'd been riding all her life. She slowed the big boy to a walk and swung off him, hitting the driveway with her reddish boots and striding toward the two men, horse trailing behind.

Her jeans were tight, her red tank top was tighter, and the brown Stetson settled on her ebony hair just iced the cake.

And yet what Adam *saw* was moonlight-drenched flesh, glistening wet and incredibly smooth. Huge shadowed eyes, parted lips, invitation. He shook the images out of his head.

"Damn good-looking gal for a city girl," Sheriff Inkwell said softly as he got to his feet. In a louder voice, he added, "Ms. De Gris, nice you could join us."

She stuck out a lightly tanned hand to shake with Inkwell. "Did I keep you waiting?" she asked, checking her wrist for a watch that wasn't there.

"Why are you late?" Adam grumbled.

"Am I?" She wrapped the horse's reins around the piece of railing, and met his gaze. "I lost track of time. I was out trying to find someone. Had something important to discuss with that someone but they kept getting away from me so I thought maybe Bagels and I could chase him down. We couldn't find him, though. Shame."

They stared at each other. Adam wanted two things. One—her to go away and never come back. Two—her to fall into his arms and make him forget how upset he was with her. Neither seemed likely. And the longer he kept her gaze, the more he wanted the second, to hell with the first.

Inkwell cleared his throat.

"Shall we?" he asked, and indicated they should sit on the bench.

Adam moved aside and let Echo take the spot he'd occupied. He settled his rear against the porch railing. A glance at Echo revealed she'd appropriated his cold drink and had taken a long swallow.

"Now, then, comfy?" the sheriff asked. "Fine. Go over it from the top, Ms. De Gris. Right from when you drove up to the house. You were driving, isn't that right?"

"Yes, I was driving. As we mentioned, Adam, Mr. Westin, has a bad shoulder." From there she reiterated everything the way Adam recalled it up to the point when they had separated. He listened carefully as she described seeing signs of a struggle through the front window, trying the knob, finding the door open, going inside, finding Garvey, grabbing the pillow and holding it over his chest wound.

Her beautiful face reflected every moment of the ordeal as though she relived it in the telling. Adam internally winced as he watched her. He'd left her alone to deal with it. He'd been so caught up in catching the bad guy, he'd abandoned her and at the Garveys of all places.

Was it possible he'd been chasing his own father?

No—

"And he died without ever regaining consciousness, is that right?" the sheriff persisted, his voice losing a little of the *aw-shucks* twang.

"No, like I said, he did regain consciousness. He tried to take my hand."

The sheriff rested his beefy forearms on his thighs, his hands clasped between his knees. He twisted his head to peer up at Echo. "See now, this is where you got a little sketchy yesterday. I had a feeling maybe he might have said something to you. Dying words, you know?"

"No," she said, but the way she said it caught Adam's attention. He stopped himself from doing a double take.

"Are you sure now, Ms. De Gris? He's lying there close to death, you must have looked like an angel to him. Didn't he say something, maybe point a dying finger?"

"No," she repeated.

She was a terrible liar. Her cheeks flushed, her gaze dropped and she swallowed air. Adam figured if he could sense it, Inkwell could.

"You're certain?"

"It was very stressful," she said, her fingers tapping

the sides of the slippery glass. "I didn't know how to help him. If he spoke, I didn't hear what he said."

Adam figured she was hedging now because she felt the weight of a lie. He swallowed some air of his own, trying to imagine what she was hiding. In light of the night before, the possibilities seemed anything but good.

The sheriff sat up again. "Well, you think about it, okay, ma'am? Sometimes a little distance can bring back a memory you didn't know you had. Get a good night's sleep and we'll talk tomorrow and maybe you'll have recalled some little thing. Might mean a lot, might not mean a damn thing. Best if you just let me be the judge."

"Of course," she said. "Um, when can I go home?"

"Go home? Oh, you mean back to California? In a few days. I'll let you know." Inkwell turned to Adam. "Now, how about you? Tell me again what happened."

Adam started his tale from the run across the field. He didn't remember anything new to add.

"How was this fellow dressed?" Inkwell asked.

"From the back? Let's see. Dark shirt, black jeans, boots."

"A hat?"

"Yeah, brown or black, regulation cowboy. And maybe a scarf or something red up around his neck."

He caught Echo's jerk as he described the clothes. Why had she reacted?

"That's good," Inkwell said, his glance straying to Echo and back. "Was he wearing a gun?"

"I didn't see one."

"But if he killed Mr. Garvey, he must have been armed."

"He must have. But he was some distance ahead of me."

"Yes. Because you stepped through the deck."

Adam caught the inflection in the sheriff's voice. "That's right, I did," he said.

"Exactly. Making it near impossible for you to catch up with the assumed murderer."

Adam stood abruptly, too anxious to stand there another second. "Are you trying to make a point of some kind, Sheriff?"

Inkwell feigned surprise. "Me? No, no, just making sure I understand. After all, you said yourself you went there because the two older sons had been harassing you about money they thought you owed that stinker Lucas. You couldn't have been too happy about paying them off."

"Maybe not. But not so unhappy that I'd plug their father."

Inkwell shook his head. "Calm down, Adam, I'm not saying you plugged anyone. I just wonder how anxious you were to chase down one of their enemies."

Adam stared hard at Inkwell which seemed to make no impression on the older man.

"What about the bag in Mr. Garvey's hand?" Echo asked.

Inkwell turned his attention to her. "Coke, just like you thought."

"Then he used drugs?"

"Don't know about that. Preliminary toxicology reports don't show any cocaine in his system and we found no other drugs in the house except a little weed that one of his boys fessed up to scoring."

"Then why was he holding it like that?"

"I suspect if you two hadn't come along, by the time I got there, it might have appeared to my poor blundering self that a drug deal had gone wrong. I would imagine the artifacts from your cave, if indeed that's where they're from, would have been long gone. Nothing but poor, dead

Willet Garvey hanging on to a bag of high-priced-escape-from-this-dreary-old-world, conclusions to be drawn."

Adam cleared his throat. "And the bullet that killed him? What kind was it?"

"A .22 caliber."

The sound of engine noises were faint but growing louder by the second. Adam glanced at his watch. A little after four. "I think the archaeologists are about to show up," he said, hoping the sheriff took the hint and left.

Echo stood so fast some of the ice jumped clear of the glass she still held. "I guess I'll see you tomorrow, Sheriff," she said quickly, sticking out one damp hand.

Inkwell sat back a bit. "Still, you folks got to admit, that leaves the question of why. Doesn't sit right, least ways, not to a country boy like me."

Echo's hand drifted back to her side. "What do you mean?"

He settled his light eyes on her. "Why kill old Willet?"

"Maybe someone wanted to steal the artifacts."

"Now, see, that's what I thought, but then the expert on such things, at least in our department, well, he took a look at what was in the box and he said that, while the relics and bones were old and in mostly decent shape, nothing there was intrinsically worth the risk of taking a life. I mean ethics aside, murder is a risky business."

"An argument between thieves," Adam suggested, aware that beside him, Echo startled. What was he missing? The engine noise was louder, too. This side of the lake if he was any judge. They'd be here in a few more minutes.

The sheriff spread his hands. "If the killer went to the Garvey house and he and Willet got in an argument that turned ugly, how is it his partner in crime happened to have a bag of cocaine he could conveniently leave behind?"

"Maybe he used drugs himself," Echo said.

The sheriff shook his head. "Never known a user to purposefully leave behind his stash. That bag was worth a pretty piece of change. Still, I suppose it's possible."

"Well, then—"

"But not likely. Which means whoever went to the Garvey house went specifically to kill Willet and to make it look like something it wasn't. Doesn't seem to me like Garvey's usual crowd has the brains or the cash reserves to come up with something like this and that makes me curious."

"Me, too," Adam said, "but the archaeologists are real close now. We need to talk about the preservation of what's left in that cave. You know what's up there, you were part of the team that handled things after Pierce's experience. Maybe the three of us could continue this... discussion...another time."

"Oh, sure," Inkwell said. "Tomorrow?"

Adam had rescheduled the doctor appointment for the insurance company. "Okay."

"Call ahead to make sure I'm there. And you come along, too, Ms. De Gris."

"We'll be there," Adam said reluctantly, watching as three ATVs came around the side of the pond, Dr. Wilcox leading the way.

The sheriff got to his feet as though it was an effort. He pulled on his cap and, hitching his hands on his ample waist, looked at the newcomers who had stopped in the drive and were getting off the motor vehicles. He cleared his throat. "Come to think of it, I think I'll ask one of them professors if they can verify the origins of that box of stuff we found on Willet's table."

Echo had grown very quiet and had moved back toward the house as if trying to shrink away. A knot twisted in Adam's gut. She'd tried to talk to him that afternoon—after conducting the team out to the cave. And right now she looked close to running for the hills.

Oh, crud. What had she done?

"Howdy, there," the sheriff called as though he was greeting guests at a hoedown. Adam conducted introductions, then the sheriff posed his question. Dr. Wilcox agreed to look at the contents of the box and compare it to what they'd found at the cave. Echo stood off to the side, watching the proceedings.

"The burial chamber is fascinating," Dr. Wilcox said. Professor Lavel, eyes hooded, remained quiet. Quite a difference from the man Adam had met that morning.

"Then you'll take it on?"

"Absolutely," she said.

Sheriff Inkwell started down the steps. "I'll get out of your way. You people have things to talk about, plans to make."

"Just a minute, Sheriff," Wilcox said. "This concerns you, as well."

"Pardon me, ma'am," Inkwell said, "I have been in that cavern before, true, but I'm no archaeologist."

"And we're not policemen." She looked pointedly at Adam as she added, "We'll be happy to process your cave as soon as the sheriff clears it."

"And what exactly am I clearing it of?" Sheriff Inkwell asked.

She turned worried eyes to him. "Murder."

Chapter Twelve

"Come again?" Inkwell sputtered.

"Assassinat," Professor Lavel said dramatically.

Echo chanced a quick look at Adam, who was staring at the French man. "What are you talking about?" he demanded and then his gaze met Echo's.

"I will show you," Professor Lavel volunteered as he flipped open his camera case. In a few steps, he was up on the porch standing between Adam and the sheriff, the camera in his hands. Echo peered at the screen through a gap between male shoulders, her hands clutching her stomach. She'd been worried about prints and now they had a body?

Whose body?

Professor Lavel had used the video mode to film the crevasse. The picture was a little dark and jumpy, but Echo could make out details of the ledge one hundred feet below the cave floor. There were visible pieces of trash, just as he and Wilcox had said, but not much, a can or two and what appeared to be a recently rumpled snack bag. There were also a few scattered human bones, dark from their long contact with the soil, and traces of woven cloth.

"It's at the rim of the ledge that plunges down even farther," the professor said.

"What is?"

And then it was on the screen. A skull.

Adam swore under his breath. "It's a burial cave! What did you expect to find?"

"Look closely," Professor Lavel said, his voice soft.

Echo peered intently as the picture zeroed in on the skull. She saw a ragged round hole in the middle of the forehead. From the absolute stillness on the porch, it was obvious every mind jumped to the same grisly conclusion.

Then Adam spoke. "Maybe the Indians drilled that hole. Didn't they used to do that when people were sick? There's a word for it."

"Trepanning," Dr. Wilcox said. "Burring a hole in the cranium to expose the dura mater. It was used in the belief it could ease or cure migraine headaches or epileptic seizures."

"Yeah, that," Adam said, and Echo managed to take a breath. There would be a logical explanation—

"Excusez," Professor Lavel said curtly. "I know the difference between a bullet hole and trepan burrs. But even if I did not, the bullet we found inside the skull would surely settle the matter, would it not? Native peoples of this age did not have firearms."

"And the bone isn't as dark as the others, indicating it hasn't been interred as long," Wilcox added.

The sheriff's voice lost its hominess as he barked, "Did you leave the skull just as you found it, Professor?"

"Oui, Monsieur, but of course."

"Can you tell if it's male or female? Young or old? Was the rest of the skeleton attached? How long has it been down there?"

Lavel shook his head. "I think perhaps there are additional bones, but not the whole skeleton. A few vertebrae, perhaps. Maybe a small *tremblement de terre* caused others to fall farther into the crevasse. As for sex, I do not know. None of the indicator bones were present."

"I disagree," Professor Wilcox said. "I went down into the crevasse after Professor Lavel returned and took a good look at the skull. I did anthropological work as a grad student that included a study of indigenous populations of this area in this time period. We did both pelvic and cranial sexing. I'm reasonably sure the skull is male."

Lavel turned to her. "You can say this without examining the pelvis?"

"Not with certainty. Not without being able to apply quadratic—"

"Doc," the sheriff interrupted. "Hold on a second. You think it might be male?"

"I think so. I'll know more when I can actually examine it. But on subjective visual assessment, that's my impression. In other words, the sexually dimorphic shape variations suggest a male. However, like I said, my work was on prehistoric indigenous Native Americans which this skull is not. I can say with some assurance that this skull is Caucasian."

Lavel cleared his throat. "I would agree with that. The orbital—"

"Folks?" the sheriff interrupted again. "Could we stay on subject here?"

"*Certainement.* Given the chance to closely examine the remains, I am sure we could approximate an age for the victim as well as an approximate date of death, *oui, madame?*" With the nod of Dr. Wilcox's dark head, Lavel added, "There are a few teeth still attached to the mandible that could aid in identification."

Inkwell snatched his phone out of his pocket. "I'll call my men."

"Professor Lavel has a previous engagement, but I

would be happy to assist you this evening," Dr. Wilcox said. "We left two students on site."

"That's fine," the sheriff said and walked away from the gathering to communicate with his office.

Adam pulled out his own cell. A few seconds later, Echo heard him say, "Cody? Better find Dad and get on back here. There's trouble out at the cave."

He put the phone away and looked at her. His expression clearly revealed he thought she'd done something to mess things up.

"Now wait just a second," she said, hands in front of her. "I didn't know a thing about a skull."

He grabbed her hands and led her away from the others. "But you wanted to talk to me after you got back today," he said, his voice low and urgent.

"Yes, but I didn't know about a body. I was worried about the garbage."

"The garbage? Hell, Echo, what are you talking about?"

"Fingerprints. I might as well admit it. I was afraid your father's prints might be on one of the cans."

"On the cans? You mean the ones they found in the crevasse? How? My father never goes there and if for some reason he did, the last thing in the world he would do is litter...." His stare deepened. "Oh, I get it. You thought maybe Dad went there to see Garvey, that the two of them sat down and drank a beer together. Snacked on a few pretzels, maybe. Hatched evil plots. Last night you had him killing Garvey and now you have him robbing his own property. Why in the world would he do that?"

She narrowed her eyes as she looked up at him. Her voice low, she tried to explain. "I knew something was wrong when the archaeologists got all quiet looking at the film. They were acting strange. I couldn't imagine what had happened and your father being there is the only thing that popped into my head and excuse me very much if I'm dense, I guess I should have thought of someone being murdered and thrown down the crevasse. How could that possibility have escaped me?"

To her amazement, he smiled. The next thing she knew, he'd put his arms around her. "Welcome back, spitfire."

"You don't like spitfires, remember?"

"I remember." He touched her hair and added, "Don't worry. This murder could have happened a hundred years ago."

"I hope so," she mumbled, detaching herself from his arms.

"If you're going to worry, I suggest you concentrate on the fact you're lying to the sheriff and he knows it," he added in a whisper.

"Lying? What do you mean?"

He lowered his head even closer this time, his lips touching her earlobe. "Willet Garvey said something before he died. What was it?"

"Why should I tell you?" she said, stalling for time to pull herself together. Despite everything—the people all around them, the tense atmosphere, her own tumultuous emotions—Adam's lips touching any part of her body created tiny tsunamis.

But he couldn't just walk back into her heart this way. She added, "I trusted you once before. It didn't work out so good."

She could tell he wasn't ready to let this go, but the sound of a truck pulling up in the yard caught everyone's attention. As it came to a roaring stop, Bagels whinnied and jumped around a bit. Adam caught the horse's bridle and calmed him as his father and Cody jumped out of the truck.

"What's going on?" Birch Westin demanded. He zeroed in on the sheriff. "What are you doing out here, Clayton?"

The sheriff gestured at Adam and Echo. "I came to talk to these two about Willet Garvey's murder."

Birch stopped advancing and all but scratched his head. "Then why aren't I still out mowing? Damn it, Adam, explain yourself."

"Let me," the sheriff said before Adam could respond. "Like I said, Birch, I came to talk about yesterday's murder but that was before the good professors came across a dead body in your cave."

Birch looked angry as he turned on Cody. "You know about this?"

Cody shook his head.

"These university people just found it," the sheriff said.

Birch snatched off his hat and almost threw it on the ground. His gaze flitted from Wilcox to Lavel. "Who the hell died in my cave?"

But it was Adam who answered. "No one knows yet, Dad. The archaeologist found parts of a skeleton down in that big rift in the floor of the burial cavern. Before you remind us that old bones are what everyone expected to find, this one has a bullet hole in the forehead."

"And the bullet is still rattling around in the skull," the sheriff added.

"Wait just a damn second," Birch said, his voice wilting. "We're still talking about my cave, aren't we?"

"No," the sheriff said. "As of right now, we're talking about my crime scene."

ECHO HADN'T SHOWN UP FOR dinner—Adam wished he'd had the brains to avoid the table, as well. When Pauline wasn't glowering at him for making trouble, his father was shooting him the evil eye. Even Uncle Pete looked a little green and Adam couldn't help but notice how often he surreptitiously glanced at Adam's father.

Right after dinner there was a knock on the front door—a rare commodity out at the ranch. Everyone who worked on Open Sky Ranch tended to just walk in through the kitchen.

Adam took a deep breath, fully expecting the cops. Instead, two familiar faces greeted him and he stepped aside to let the duo enter. "What are you guys doing here?" Birch asked as he came into the foyer from the dining room. He was followed by Cody who was trailed by Bonnie, as usual.

"Is it true what we heard?" Del Halverson asked, his face more flushed than ever as though he'd run the twenty miles between their ranches instead of traveling it in the big blue SUV that sat right outside.

"I don't know. What did you hear?" Adam asked.

J. D. Oakes stood at Halverson's side, smoothing his mustache, his keen eyes bright and watchful. A few years before people had urged Oakes to run for mayor of Woodwind, but he'd declined. Claimed he came to ranching a little later than some and was having too much fun being a cowboy to mess about in politics. He said, "Seems one of the students who was out here today has a big mouth and spread the word about your dead body."

"Hell, it's not our dead body," Birch said. "Who knows how old that skeleton is? My money is on hanky-panky dating back before my grandfather's time."

"Do the cops know who it is?" Oakes asked.

"Not yet."

"Suppose they'll have to investigate."

"Yeah."

"What I want to know," Halverson said, "is why you

never mentioned that cave had remains and artifacts in there."

"I didn't tell many people but I could have sworn I told you two. Melissa was the only one who ever went there. Said she found it peaceful."

"I don't remember you saying a thing," Halverson insisted.

"I don't, either," Oakes said.

Birch shrugged. "Must have been over thirty years ago. Maybe I didn't. Hell, who can remember, we're all getting old. Speaking of which, where's Lonnie? He called here before dinner. Said he was coming on out to talk to me tomorrow. Either of you fellows know what that's about?"

Halverson darted a swift look at J.D. but he shook his head. "He's been acting squirrelly. The Garvey murder really got under his skin."

"Lonnie is the high-strung type," Oakes added. "The sheriff say anymore about suspects in the Garvey murder?"

"Not a thing, leastways not to me."

Adam shook his head as all the others' eyes slid to him. "Nothing."

Halverson's small features bunched together even tighter as though he'd gotten a whiff of something foul. "You better know I heard talk some people think you killed Willet Garvey 'cause he was stealing from you, Birch."

Oakes snorted. "What a bunch of malarkey."

Halverson nodded. "I'm thinking Lonnie has something to get off his chest."

Adam tensed. "What do you mean?"

Halverson's gaze once again darted to J.D. and then back. "Nothing. Not my place to get into this. If Lonnie has something to tell you, he'll do it on his own time."

"No doubt it's why he wants to see you," J.D. added.

Birch swore softly. "I don't like all this sneaky stuff. Give me cattle and fresh air and a real job. Which reminds me, Adam, sometime in the next few days, you need to go take a look at the fences up at the Hayfork field. Mike said they need attention."

"Sure," Adam said. Like his father, he, too, liked a chore he could do with his own hands.

"Hell, I need a drink," Birch mumbled.

"You gonna let me smoke in your office?" J.D. asked, patting his chest pocket to make sure he had his tobacco and papers.

"If you sit by an open window," Birch said reluctantly. The three older men trooped into the office in gloomy silence, followed by Pete. Adam hadn't even noticed his uncle had joined the group.

Cody caught Adam's eye. His lowered his voice. "You have any idea who's in that blasted cave?"

"None. You?"

"Yeah. One."

"Who?"

"That ranch hand Dad thought was carrying on with Mom."

Adam looked over his shoulder to make sure no one was listening. Still, the direction this conversation was taking begged for privacy. He opened the front door and strode outside, Cody right behind him, Bonnie darting ahead. They shoved their hands in their pockets as the door slammed at their backs. When Adam spoke, his voice was soft. "David Lassiter? You're kidding."

"Think about it. Eight or nine years after Lassiter disappeared and we were old enough to be out on our own, Dad forbade us to go into the burial cavern. What if he shot David Lassiter and pushed him into that hole? What if that's why Mom left here?"

This was too much. The day before, Echo had more or less accused their father of killing Willet Garvey and now Cody had him murdering David Lassiter. Hell, even their friends were passing along rumors. Adam stared at his brother as though he were a stranger. "Do you honestly think Dad is capable of something like that?"

"I think any man is with the right provocation."

"Jealousy?"

Cody nodded. "What happened between Cassie and me was strictly between us, but if there'd been some other guy, well, I don't know. I might have gone after the bastard."

"This is nuts," Adam said.

Cody pinned him with his dark gaze. "You don't feel like that about Echo?"

"Now wait just a second—"

"Come on, Adam. Like you said, I live here. You think I can't see what's going on?"

"I've known her for three friggin' days," Adam protested. "Give me a break."

Cody gazed into his eyes an extra beat. "Well, I spent years playing games, too. Who am I to judge?" He took a deep breath before adding, "What's going on with Lonnie, J.D. and Del? They're all acting like they have a big secret."

Adam was happy to turn the conversation away from him and Echo. "Who knows? Think it's important?"

"I'd say, about now, any secret is a potential time bomb, wouldn't you?"

Chapter Thirteen

Adam left Solar Flare in his stall where the horse was already tucked in for the night. He needed to walk and think and try to figure out if he was too close to the forest to see the trees. He headed home on foot.

It was a beautiful night but it couldn't begin to compare to the one before when he'd come this way with Echo riding behind him. It was impossible not to wonder what life was going to be like around here when the sheriff gave her permission to leave. Fact was, he wasn't even sure what a television producer did, especially one on a channel devoted to food.

Be reasonable—what would a woman like her want a guy like him for? He couldn't give her the razzle-dazzle excitement of a city or a job she loved. His life was as tied to the land he walked upon as it was to the air he breathed and all of it was one-hundred-percent Wyoming.

She was wrong for him. He was wrong for her. Did he want to spend the rest of his life waiting for her to leave him like Cody had with Cassie? Hell, no. Running after her, wearing his heart on his sleeve? Again, hell no.

And that's when he saw her, walking toward him, a slim figure in the fading light. It appeared she had walked around the lake. He didn't think she'd noticed him yet. Her head was down, she looked contemplative. He could take a few steps to his right and be on top of the ridge in thirty seconds and she need never know he was there.

And yet she was keeping a secret about Willet Garvey's last words and in light of everything that had happened, he needed to man up and find out what she knew.

It couldn't be good. That much was clear.

Eventually, she turned her head and saw him. He stepped up his pace and they soon met on the moonlit path.

"What are you doing out here?" he asked.

"Just walking. Thinking. You know."

"Avoiding me?"

"Not everything is about you," she grumbled. "I saw a truck arrive a while ago. More trouble?"

"No, just some of Dad and Uncle Pete's buddies, out to offer support. You met them the first day you arrived."

She crinkled her brow, then nodded. "Kind of a pink man and a guy with a Colonel Sanders mustache?"

"Right."

They were silent for a moment until Adam spoke. "You know, I was wondering what a television producer actually does."

She looked up at him quickly.

He added, "You're not in front of the camera, right?"

"No."

"Do you tell people what to do?"

She shrugged.

"Come on, just tell me. I'm curious."

"You're curious? Why?"

"Why not? Give me the short version."

"The short version. Well, in my case, I work for the station. I'm the one who's responsible for getting things done on time. I oversee hiring directors and talent and take care of the bottom line."

"Making it pay."

"Yes. Well, in a way. It's my responsibility to turn a profit for the investors. Isn't that what all business is about at the end of the day?"

"Yeah. But it seems a shame to waste a face and figure like yours behind the camera."

Her eyes flashed to his and away. He'd half expected her to call him out on making that kind of quasi sexist remark, but she let it slide with a soft, "It's what I find interesting."

"You must be looking forward to New York."

She met his gaze again and then looked out at the lake. "I'll miss all my friends and coworkers in San Francisco, of course."

"Then why are you leaving?"

"It's what you do in a career, right? Keep advancing higher up the ladder, take on more challenges, all that."

"I suppose. Do you know anyone in New York?"

"Not yet."

"It sounds kind of lonely to me."

"Doesn't anyone ever leave here?"

"You mean Wyoming?" he asked, picking up a handful of rocks and lobbing one into the dark lake. The noise reminded him of the playful splashes of the night before. He dropped the rest of the rocks to the ground and brushed the dirt off his hands. "Sure. Pierce left for years."

"This brother of yours sounds interesting. I don't remember much about him except he thought I was irritating."

"Heck, Echo, we all thought you were irritating."

She laughed softly. "Well, as far as I can see, Pierce is the only one around here who tackled the world outside Wyoming."

"Some of my college friends have moved away. And those men you met, Dad's buddies. Like Del Halverson."

"The pink one. But he came back."

"His uncle ran a bank in Jersey, gave Del a job. Del said the desk-jockey thing got old after a while."

"And the other one?"

"J. D. Oakes. He grew up in Montana, made a mint in the mining business, settled here and became a gentleman rancher. Lonnie is the one you didn't meet. He's been around forever, but now that you mention it, he left when he was drafted and didn't come back for almost five years."

She looked up at him again. "But not you."

"Hell, honey, I'm the world's last content man. I know what I have and what I want."

"Do you?" she said softly.

He didn't really think it was a question so he didn't answer it.

"What do you do all winter?"

"Work on my house. And I have hobbies—the guitar, painting, woodcarving. Then there are social things at the Grange, get-togethers with old friends. Plus ranching just slows down, you know, it doesn't quit. There are still chores to do, animals to tend and if there isn't some remote fence that needs work, then it's damn near a miracle." He darted a glance at her. "Probably sounds pretty boring to you." He waited a second before adding, "What would you do if you weren't in television?"

"I'd go into medicine," she said quickly, flicking him a glance, perhaps to see if he thought the answer was amusing.

"Really?"

"Yeah. After my recent experiences around here, it's kind of hit me that I would like to know what to do in an emergency. I don't like feeling helpless when a life is at stake."

He smiled down at her, wishing so much he could cup her face and kiss her. Forever. Nonstop.

She looked up at him again, the whites of her eyes glistening. "Will you show me the inside of your house?"

"Sure."

"Now?"

He paused as he tried to figure out how big a mess he'd left the last time he had spent any time there. When was that, anyway? Two nights ago?

"If the sheriff gives his okay, I'll be leaving tomorrow," she added.

"As long as you don't mind a few dirty dishes," he said, "I'd be happy to give you the grand tour."

It wasn't a long walk, but once in a while the trail sloped and they brushed hands or arms. The difference between their level of physical intimacy from the night before to this night was downright gut-wrenching.

"I'm glad you brought up the fact you might be leaving soon," he said as they neared his house.

"Why? Anxious to be rid of me?"

"You know better than that. But you're never going to get out of here until you tell Sheriff Inkwell the truth. Don't underestimate him. He'll keep you here until doomsday if he thinks you're holding back."

Her hand landed on his arm and he looked down at her, his heart hammering in his chest. It wasn't just because he was so worried about what she'd heard Garvey say. His whole body burned with the desire to pick her up and carry her into his house. He could smell her, taste her…

She took a shallow breath and lowered her voice. "What if what I heard lays suspicion where you don't want it?"

"I guess that's just the way it has to be, Echo. No matter

what Willet said, Dad didn't kill him. Even if he'd gone there, he wouldn't have brought drugs along because he doesn't do drugs. I doubt he has the slightest idea how to even score any. That would mean premeditation and that's not my father's style. He blows up fast and then cools down. Tell the sheriff what you know."

"Don't you want me to tell you first?" she asked as they climbed the steps leading to the covered front porch. It was very dark under the overhang. He needed to buy one of those motion sensor lights.

With one hand on the doorknob, he paused. "Of course I want to know, but maybe you should just tell Inkwell. I disappointed you once before."

"Oh, Adam, it's all so complicated, isn't it?"

He kissed her forehead and thought about inching south to her lips. And face it, there was a great big soft bed one short flight of stairs away....

"Willet touched my arm," she said softly. "He said, 'Westin. Tell Den...hat... Westin...' and then he died."

"Hat? What did that mean?"

"I didn't know for sure but then—"

"Let me enlighten you," a low voice interrupted as a figure emerged from the deep shadows of the porch. The man carried a shotgun in one hand and grabbed the railing for support when his step faltered. "It means he saw you hanging around, wearing that black hat of yours... watching him. I don't know how you did it, but you killed my dad."

Heavy footsteps sounded from the stairs behind while at the same time, the front door flew open and the lights snapped on.

Adam pulled Echo against his side as the three remaining Garvey brothers closed in around them.

DENNIS GARVEY STOOD INSIDE Adam's house, hands twitching at his sides, eyes darting between the older guys standing on either side of her and Adam.

The biggest and apparently the oldest of the two wore a scraggly dark beard and a black shirt. Pearl buttons glittered on his chest. He had pit-bull eyes and even from a foot away, reeked of alcohol. Echo placed him at about her own age.

The other one looked to be a couple years younger. He wore facial hair, too, but in his case, it appeared to be more a consequence of poor grooming. His eyes had a fevered, drunken look to them and he, too, smelled like a brewery.

Adam directed his comments to the bearded man. "Hank. What are you and Tommy and Dennis doing here?"

"Waiting for you," Hank said, hoisting the shotgun with both hands. "Been waiting for you since the wee hours of the morning."

"You didn't come home last night," Dennis said, almost as an accusation. He flashed a look at Echo that seemed half defiance and half apology.

"You didn't think we was going to let you get away with murdering our daddy, did you?" the shabby brother who had to be Tommy said.

"I didn't hurt your father. There are lots of people who saw me other places."

"Like her?" Tommy said, pointing at Echo.

"I'm one of them," Echo said, "but not the only one."

"You're forgetting I just heard you tell him what Daddy said with his last breath," Hank said. He repeated the words for Dennis's sake. The repetition wasn't exact and was slurred, but it came across loud and clear anyway. Dennis's hands curled into fists.

"Let the lady walk on back to the ranch," Adam said. "Then we'll go inside and get a cold drink. Talk this over like men."

"You ain't got no more cold drinks," Tommy said and laughed. He rubbed the back of his hand across his mouth. "We drank your beer, every last one. Time to break out the hard stuff."

"The lady ain't going nowhere," Hank said.

"She has nothing to do with any of this," Adam said. "It doesn't concern her."

Dennis glanced at Echo again. "I say we let her go. We don't got no beef with her."

"Don't be silly. I'm not leaving," Echo said firmly as she gazed up at Adam. Didn't he know her at all? Did he really think she'd leave him alone?

He gazed directly into her eyes and she realized what an idiot she was being. If she left, she could summon help. Two drunks and a shotgun were nothing to be taken lightly.

"On second thought, this isn't my battle, I'd only get in the way," she said. "I'll just—"

"You're staying right where you are!" Hank yelled, drops of spittle landing on his beard. "You're related. Maybe not by way of blood, but you're a Westin just the same."

Tommy pushed them both into the house. Echo stumbled on the threshold and Adam caught her. The suppressed tension in his body traveled through his hands and up her arms.

The door slammed behind them.

Dennis ran around the big room turning on lights. As he did, different spaces were illuminated and each was more breathtaking than the one before. Too scared to take in details, Echo was left with impressions of warm wood and lots of glass.

And then the stench of stale beer and half-eaten food hit her olfactory glands. Tommy lurched over to the table in front of a red leather sofa and picked up a can. He drained what was in it, then threw it across the room.

The clatter it made as it hit the wall caused Echo to jump.

"What do you guys want?" Adam demanded, jaw knotted, silver eyes the color of pewter.

"I want to be staring you in the eyes when you die, just like you did our dad," Hank said, his voice garbled, tears rolling down his cheeks unheeded.

"I didn't kill your father," Adam said softly.

Tommy had moved off toward what appeared to be the kitchen. He returned a minute later carrying two bottles, one of whiskey, the other of gin. He opened the gin and took a long swallow before offering the bottle to Hank who waved it away.

"Wait a second," Dennis said. He was standing with his hands on the back of the sofa, looking at the rest of them like they were actors on a stage. "No matter which Westin pulled the trigger, you can bet his pa set up our dad."

Hank stared hard at Adam, then he swore. "Damn it, Den, you're right." He nosed the gun closer to Adam. "Call your old man," he demanded. "Get him over here."

"So you can shoot both of us?" Adam said calmly. "I don't think so."

Hank leered at Echo. "I'll shoot her if you don't call them."

"No, you won't. She hasn't done you any harm. All she did was try to comfort your dad."

"That's right," Dennis said, voice cracking.

With a sweep of his arm, Tommy cleared empty beer cans and stale sandwich crusts off the low table by the sofa. The whiskey bottle hit the wood with a clink while Tommy upended the gin and swilled down another inch. Then he jerked his head toward the front of the house.

"Do you hear something?"

Hank didn't take his eyes off Adam. They were all silent for a second. All Echo could hear was the drumming of her own erratic heart.

Hank finally said, "No."

"Well, I do," Tommy muttered, and lurched toward the window, cradling the bottle against his chest. "See, I was right!" he yelled. "There are lights coming down the road." He turned back to the room, waving the bottle. "Someone's coming. We got to get out of here."

Hank thrust the shotgun closer to Adam. Echo stopped breathing. The muzzle was less than a foot from Adam's chest.

"Hank, don't, you're drunk!" Dennis cried.

Adam took a deep breath. Then, his movements lightning-quick, he grabbed the barrel of the shotgun and yanked it to the side. Hank was unsteady enough to stumble forward but his finger was still on the trigger. The gun went off.

Echo screamed, certain Adam had taken a bullet.

But it was Tommy who crumpled to the floor. He grabbed his bloody left leg as the gin bottle exploded beside him. Within seconds, the man was lying in a puddle of his own blood mixed liberally with booze.

While Hank stared at his brother, Adam landed a punch on his nose. Hank reeled back in the other direction, toward Echo, rounding himself up, reaching for her with hands like claws, his small eyes burning with rage. She grabbed the whiskey bottle from the table and holding the neck with both her hands, thumped Hank over the head so hard the action jarred her arms and she dropped the bottle. It burst on the rock floor in a spurting fountain of amber spirits and glass.

Hank stared at her with crossed eyes before crashing at her feet.

She looked up at Adam. He stood cradling his arm, his expression taut with pain. He'd used the wrong hand to slug Hank Garvey.

Echo was barely able to process the last sixty seconds and the fact that she and Adam were still standing and relatively unhurt. Then she looked around for Dennis and found him kneeling at Tommy's side.

"Is he okay?" she asked.

Dennis had whipped off a light jacket and was holding it against his brother's leg. He glanced up. "He's so drunk he probably don't even know he's been shot."

A moment later, Cody and Sheriff Inkwell walked into the house.

Chapter Fourteen

The ambulance crew took Tommy out on a stretcher. Sheriff Inkwell's deputies hauled off Hank and Dennis. Dennis, who was a minor, wouldn't face the same charges as his more aggressive brothers but as Adam watched the boy get into the squad car, he felt more than just a pang of regret.

In the Westin family, at least in this generation, his brother Pierce had been the one who got himself in all sorts of trouble as a teen. In fact, their father had grown so annoyed with Pierce's repeated run-ins with the law that he'd thrown him off the ranch. Pierce hadn't come home for more than a visit in the fifteen years following that event. It was only a couple months ago when he'd really rejoined the family.

But maybe Pierce had managed to pull himself out of his downward spiral because he'd had a strong family behind him with expectations that he would find his way. That was something that Dennis didn't have and likely never would. How would a kid like that ever get a decent break, especially around here where his family's menfolk were legends—and not the good kind?

Adam realized he'd been staring after the ambulance doing what his grandfather used to call woolgathering.

He tried rolling his bad shoulder and found the pain had subsided. He went back inside.

He found Echo and Cody down on the floor carefully picking up pieces of broken glass and depositing them in a metal bucket.

The sheriff had also stayed behind and was standing with his back to the room, gazing out the window toward the dark lake beyond. The fact he hadn't gone with his men seemed ominous to Adam.

The house smelled terrible. Adam left the door open to let in what little air stirred the summer night. On further thought, he crossed the large room and opened the patio doors. Might as well try to catch a cross breeze.

Then he looked at the sheriff. "How did you and Cody just happen to show up when you did?"

"Pure coincidence," Inkwell said.

Cody dropped the neck of the broken bottle into the bucket as he looked up from his chore. "The sheriff came to the house after you left. I was still outside. He asked me to come over here with him."

"What about Dad and Uncle Pete—"

"I'll talk to them later," Inkwell said. "Wanted a chance to talk to you two first. Alone."

"Should I leave?" Echo asked.

"No, Ms. De Gris, I think you should stay."

Adam's gut seized for about the tenth time that evening. How many times in her short visit had Echo's life been threatened, and mostly because of him? He caught her gaze. Her eyes looked a little glassy.

"Are you okay?" he asked.

"I think I'm getting a buzz from the fumes."

He offered her his good hand and pulled her to her feet. "I'll finish this later. Let's hear what the sheriff has to say." He led the way to the dining alcove. It was far enough removed from the living area that the air was a little less toxic.

Inkwell sat in the chair at the head of the table Adam had finished last winter. He'd crafted it out of a single slab of hand-planed black walnut, carving Wyoming state's flower, the Indian paintbrush, on each massive supporting leg. A hint of dark orange stain went on the flowers then lots of varnish so the design all but disappeared unless you knew to look for it.

The sheriff gazed pointedly at Echo, who sat to his right with Adam on her other side. Cody sat across from them.

"You should be aware, Ms. De Gris," Inkwell began, "that Hank Garvey was ranting and raving as we arrested him. I gather from his gibberish that you've finally recalled what his father said. Would you share that with me, please, or should I wait until Hank sobers up and have a go at him?"

Echo took a deep breath. Her left hand rested right beside Adam's on the bench seat and he covered her fingers with his. "No, I'll tell you," she said, her voice shaking. "Willet Garvey did have dying words and I did hear them. He said, 'Westin. Tell Den…hat… Westin…' I didn't see how it could do anything but incite everyone so I decided to keep it to myself. When Adam figured out I wasn't being truthful with you, he insisted I come clean. I was going to tell you. I'm sorry I lied."

The sheriff sat back and sighed. "Well, now, that wasn't so bad, was it?" He sounded like a big old teddy bear. Adam didn't buy it for a minute but Echo smiled, relief evident on her face.

And yet…

She'd been about to add something else when Hank Garvey interrupted her. He met her gaze and she looked away so quickly it was hard to believe no one else saw she was still equivocating. Uh-oh...

Cody thumped the table with a fist. "We all know Adam couldn't have killed Willet."

"Well, now, he isn't the only Westin, is he?" said the sheriff. "There's your pa and your uncle and your brother Pierce and then there's you."

"Pierce is half a world away. Besides, none of us would—"

"'Course you wouldn't," the sheriff interrupted. "Let's just leave that for now. But the word *hat* is a little odd, isn't it?"

"Tell us about the cave," Adam said. "Did you figure out who's down there?"

The sheriff's smile slid away as he reached into his shirt pocket. He took out a small brown bag and carefully slid something glittery into his hand.

Cody and Adam both gasped.

ECHO LOOKED FROM ONE BROTHER to the other. "What is it?"

It was a dumb question. The object's identity was obvious. A locket, constructed of what appeared to be a mother-of-pearl oval ringed with diamonds, a little bigger than a quarter, a gold chain puddled around it.

"May I?" Cody whispered as he stretched out his hand. The sheriff handed it over very gently.

"Is it hers?" Adam asked. Echo had never heard that tone in his voice before.

Cody swallowed hard and nodded.

"Whose?" Echo asked, although as soon as the word left her mouth, her memory flashed back to a winter day when she was very small. Her mother had been ill, bed-bound actually, but Echo sat cradled on a woman's lap, sitting in front of a fire, drowsy and too warm, her fingers curled around something smooth, something that glowed and twinkled at the same time.

The woman sang to her, smoothed her hair....

Aunt Melissa...

"It's your mother's locket, isn't it?"

Cody turned it over in his hand. He studied the back of the gold case for a second, closed his eyes, then handed it to Adam. Echo saw the initials *MBW* scrolled in the gold on the back of the case. *Melissa Browning Westin*.

Adam flicked it open with a fingernail. A young Birch Westin stared up from one side of the locket looking so much like Adam that Echo gulped. Three tiny boys grinned into the camera on the second side.

Cody's voice, when he spoke, was reflective. "Dad gave her this locket on their wedding day."

Adam cleared his throat. "Where did you find it?" He snapped the locket shut. Echo held out her hand and he passed it to her. It felt smooth and warm to the touch, just as she remembered.

"I got something to tell you boys," the sheriff began, and his voice held a compassionate note that chilled Echo to the bone. "We found your mother's locket down in the deepest part of that chasm. It was there along with a lot of other bones. I guess that French fellow was right. An earthquake must have shook the first body apart, leaving the skull and some random bones on the uppermost ledge. The others fell down to the bottom."

"The first body?" Adam said, leaning forward. "What do you mean?"

"There's no easy way to say this." He took a deep breath. "It's true there's a man's skull with a bullet hole in the head on the first ledge. But there's another skeleton down at the bottom along with some rotting clothes. I'm sorry, but that locket was still around the neck of the second skeleton."

Echo's hand flew to cover her mouth. Beside her, Adam stiffened.

Cody's eyes narrowed. "I don't get it. What are you saying? That our mother is in that cave? That she's been there all these years?"

"Dr. Wilcox said we won't know for sure until we get her dentist to compare ante-mortem and postmortem dental records, but that's the way it looks right now."

Adam stood abruptly. "This is crazy. It's impossible. We got a postcard from her from Toronto. Ask Dad, ask Uncle Pete."

"I plan to," Inkwell said softly.

ADAM SAT IN A CHAIR IN THE living room of his father's house, his mind drifting from one disaster to the next. The sheriff was using the office phone, his father was next door rousing Pete. The clock on the mantel reported it was two-fifteen. For a second he tried to remember the last time he'd had a full night's sleep and couldn't.

She was here all the time. She never left.

Echo perched on the edge of the big square coffee table and offered him a red mug. "It's herbal tea," she said softly as though there'd been a death in the family and the house was one of mourning.

Which was exactly on point.

He took the tea, had a sip. It tasted like brewed weeds. "Thanks," he said.

"You're welcome." She leaned forward and ran her warm fingers down his cheek. "I'm so sorry."

"I know."

"In a way, though, isn't this a good thing?"

Leave it to Echo to shake him out of himself. He furrowed his brow as he set the cup on an end table. "A good thing? How do you see that?"

"Well, your mother didn't really run out on your family."

He took her hands in his and lowered his voice in case the sheriff came into the room. "Listen to me. Someone apparently killed my mother and the man she was rumored to be running around with. His has got to be that skull with the bullet hole. Someone buried both of them in a cave that not many people knew about. Take a guess at who is going to be suspect number one. Her husband, that's who. My father."

"Oh, Adam," she said, clutching his hands. "All along you've been convinced he was incapable of murder. Don't give up on him now."

"I won't," he said and hoped he could live up to that conviction.

She squeezed his hands and released them. "Where's Cody?"

"Rummaging around in the attic. He said he wanted to look for a picture of Mom. He's the oldest, you know, he has the most memories of her. To me she was just a shadow. Sometimes I almost hated her. And all the time she was rotting away at the bottom of that damn cave."

Echo wiped a tear from her own cheek.

"I want you to leave as soon as you can," he said softly.

"But—"

"Promise me. You've cheated death over and over again since you got here. The two older Garveys are in jail and Dennis seems like a decent kid, but he'll bend to the will of his brothers. It's not safe here."

"You've been in more danger than I have."

"This mess is my mess, not yours. I can't walk away. You can."

The familiar flash of annoyance sparkled in her eyes. "Okay, I get it. You don't need me. Message received. But maybe I have other reasons for sticking around. Have you ever thought of that?"

"Does that reason include the fact you're still hiding something about Willet Garvey's death?"

She opened her mouth and closed it. The room was suddenly full of people. The sheriff came out of the den at the same time Adam's father and uncle burst through the connecting kitchen door. Pauline arrived a moment later and for once, she looked all of her sixty-plus years.

"So, Clayton, you hauling me off to jail?" Birch Westin snarled as the sheriff tucked his cap under his arm.

"You know I'm not. There's still a lot to do out at that cave. I just want you two to go over what happened the night Melissa went missing."

"Hell, I told you decades ago," Birch grumbled. "Several times, as I recall."

"I was a new deputy at the time. Refresh my memory."

"Do you know for sure it's her?" Pete asked. He looked gray and unbelievably weary. "Do you know it's Melissa?"

"Not for sure. We will by tomorrow, though. Birch said her dentist is still practicing in Woodwind."

"Let's get this over with," Birch said.

The sheriff gestured at the massive leather furniture. "Let's sit down—"

"No thanks," Birch said. He folded his arms across his chest. "I'm fine just like this."

"Suit yourself," Inkwell said. "Me? I'm bushed." He sank into a wingback chair and settled his hat on his knee while Uncle Pete took the companion chair. Pauline leaned with her back against the wall, well out of the way.

"Go on," the sheriff coaxed. "This is informal, just refresh me. Unless you want your lawyer present."

"Are you charging me?" Birch snapped.

"No, no. Just advising you. Go on."

The old man rubbed his face with his hand and took a deep breath. "It's no secret Melissa and I had a fight the night she left."

"About?"

"Nothing important. The usual stuff." He started pacing. "We'd had a party. It was after market and we were all happy to see the end of a difficult season. Melissa loved parties. She got a little tipsy. Hell, we both did. After the house emptied out, we got to fighting."

"What about?"

"I don't know. Me telling the same jokes for the hundredth time, her flirting with Del and J.D., something, anything."

"If I remember correctly, you said at the time it turned into a screaming match."

"She could make me insane, I don't deny that. Never met a woman like her. One minute you wanted to kiss her, the next you wanted to throttle her."

His words hung there like a self-indictment.

Birch looked around the room, his gaze falling on Pete. "Hell, you know what I mean. You were in love with her, too. So were half the men in the county."

Adam stared at his uncle, who had dropped his gaze to his hands. Echo was watching him, too, her expressive eyes narrowed.

The sheriff finally spoke again. "Melissa was rumored to be carrying on with David Lassiter."

"Melissa knew the difference between flirting and adultery."

"But did Lassiter?"

Birch shrugged. "He was a good-looking guy, real chatty. They just seemed to hit it off."

"Did you fight over her attentions to him?"

Birch glared down at Inkwell. "He wasn't even at the party."

"But before that night had you fought about David Lassiter?"

"I don't know, I don't remember. What matters is the night she disappeared and that fight wasn't about any one man. I lost my temper, she stormed off. She'd done that before. Earlier that year she was gone for a whole month and during calving season, too."

"But this time she didn't return."

"No."

"And you didn't try to find her?"

"Hell, no. If she needed to blow off steam, I figured *let her*. I knew she'd come home. She always did. She'd left three little kids here. Four, if you count Echo whose own mother was sickly."

"And when she didn't return? What then?"

"I called you. You people came out here and more or less accused me of doing something terrible to her or do you forget that?"

"No, I remember. By then we'd gotten word David Lassiter was missing, too. Sounded mighty fishy."

"He was a drifter. Men like him came and went with the wind. Hell, three of them left without notice that year. Near as I could tell, he never planned on staying around for long."

"Yeah, that's what you said. We never could find any of his family."

"Actually, a guy came by a few months later, claimed to be Lassiter's cousin."

The sheriff furrowed his brow. "I don't remember hearing about that."

"By then we'd heard from Melissa and you guys were no longer hounding me."

"What did this cousin want?"

"He said he hadn't heard from Lassiter since receiving a letter back when he worked on the Open Sky. Wanted to know if I could help find him. I couldn't so he went on his way."

"Did he leave you a name or an address?"

"I don't remember. By then I'd—I'd given up on my wife. I'd decided to go on without her. If she'd made a new life, what was I supposed to do about it?"

"Did you ever try to track her down?"

"Run after her? Hell, no. A man has his pride."

Adam looked away from the raw pain in his father's eyes.

"Let me ask you this, Birch. She didn't take her purse or her wallet or any clothes—how did that make sense to you?"

"It didn't," he said.

"Unless," the sheriff offered, "she took off steaming mad and refused to return for her stuff so she wouldn't have to see you. But for that to work, she would have had to be with someone else, someone with money and a car—someone like Lassiter."

Birch shook his head. Adam finally realized the truth of the sheriff's observation and also that his father had apparently denied this basic truth for nearly three decades.

Inkwell turned to Adam's uncle. "How about you?"

Pete's shoulders jerked. "Me and my family were living out in the old house our parents raised us in," he began. "It's been torn down since then. I didn't know Melissa was gone until the next morning. I'm not sure when Lassiter took off. It was the end of the season, the time when drifters tended to move on and they often didn't tell anyone."

"It never crossed your mind they'd gone away together?"

Adam caught Pete's swift glance at Birch before he said, "No."

The sheriff turned back to Adam's father. "Tell me about the postcard."

His dad was on the move again, taking jerky steps back and forth in front of the fireplace. "What do you want to know? The picture was of some building up there in Toronto. The message was in Melissa's handwriting and it said the same thing she'd said before. She needed space. She loved me and the kids."

"Did she say she was never coming back?" the sheriff asked.

"No. Time just kept passing...."

"Do you still have the postcard?"

"Heck, I don't know. I doubt it." He stopped abruptly in his tracks. "My God, if it's really Melissa down in the cave, who sent that card?"

Adam had almost forgotten about Pauline, but as his father's question hung in the air, he heard her soft intake of breath. He looked up to find she'd gripped the back of a chair for support. Her eyes were closed, her mouth was a tight line.

The sheriff stood up and pulled on his hat as though getting ready for a quick getaway. "Now, that's what I call a very interesting question." His gaze shifted from Birch to Pete and back again. "Any ideas?"

Both men looked quickly away.

Chapter Fifteen

The sheriff left soon after that. In his wake, the occupants of the log house sat in desultory silence, no one looking directly at anyone else.

"We should try to get some sleep," Adam's father finally said. He had seated himself on the other sofa and Pauline had perched beside him.

Cody came down the stairs at last, a small box clutched in his hands, his dog on his heels. "Did the sheriff leave already?"

"You just missed him," Adam said. Echo stirred at the sound of his voice and he realized she'd all but fallen asleep sitting there beside him. With a flash of desire so strong it rocked him, he wanted to take her in his arms and hold her through the night, protect her from all this.

Cody sat down on a chair close to his father. Bonnie curled up nearby, her chin on his boots. He put the box on the table in front of them. "Do you remember this, Dad?"

The box had held El Roi-Tan cigars back in the day. It was about five by seven inches, two inches deep, made of thick paper with boldly printed words and design. The lid lifted on one long side, the two original paper seals on either end long broken. Presently, a rubber band held it securely closed.

Birch gripped his knees with his hands. "I'd all but forgotten about it. Did you open it?"

"Yeah. It was in a trunk in the attic. I was looking for old photographs of Mom, but this was all I found."

"That's all there is," their father said. "That's all that's left."

"It's yours," Cody said.

Birch picked up the box, stared at it a moment, then handed it to Adam. "I remember pretty much what's in there," he said. "It's not much, I'll tell you that. Not much…"

Adam slipped off the rubber band and folded back the lid. His father hadn't been kidding when he said there wasn't much.

The topmost item was a photograph of his parents' wedding, his mother in a lacy white dress, his father in a Western-styled suit. His mother's father had been governor of Wyoming at the time and he stood beside his daughter sporting a campaign smile. The only other person in the photo was his dad's mother, Grandma Opal, who wore a dress it appeared she'd made herself.

Echo leaned over him to gaze at the photo. She touched the hollow of his mother's throat where the twinkle of diamonds surrounded a small, pale pendant. "The locket," she whispered.

"It was my wedding gift to her," Birch said softly. "Her father had given her a locket when she was a teenager but she'd given it to Analise's mother when they shared a room at college. So, I gave her that one."

"Analise brought Grandpa's locket back when she came to visit," Adam said. "It's upstairs."

Adam gazed at his mother's face another moment or two. She looked a lot like Echo. Same dark hair and snapping eyes, same athletic figure and the buzz of energy that somehow managed to transcend paper and ink to say nothing of decades.

He set it aside to uncover a postcard of a big red brick building labeled Union Station, Toronto, Canada. Turning it over, he read, "Darling—You know me, I need a little more time. Thank Pauline for covering for me. Kiss my babies." It was signed with a capital *M* and postmarked three weeks after his mother had left the house that October night.

"What does she mean about thanking Pauline for covering for her? You mean here at the house?"

Pauline answered. "I don't remember, do you, Birch?"

"Not exactly. It must have been the house. You were still married to Ernie then and coming here twice a week to help except when Melissa left the ranch and you came more often."

Pauline nodded gently. She looked beyond weary.

"Is this her handwriting?" he asked.

It was Pete who spoke up. "Yeah, I recognize it, don't you, Birch?"

Birch grunted his assent.

Under the postcard were three more pictures, each of his mother holding one of her sons as babies. In his own, his mother was about his age now and the mother-of-pearl locket glowed against her tanned skin. He pushed the photo aside.

All that remained were a few old letters postmarked Chatioux, letters sent from Pierce's bride's mother, now the queen of Chatioux, way back before she'd married the king.

Adam put everything back inside and closed the lid. "I think we need to give the postcard to the sheriff," he said.

"Why would he want it?" Pete asked, his voice gravelly with fatigue.

"It's evidence. He asked about it. We can't withhold anything."

His father waved his hand.

"I'll put it in an envelope and take it with me tomorrow," Adam added as he opened the box again, withdrew the card and put the box back on the table.

"I shouldn't have gotten rid of everything," Birch said. "I should have tried to find her. I was just so sure she'd had enough of me. I was so disappointed in her for running out on you guys."

Adam leaned forward and met his father's eyes. "I know you didn't hurt Mom."

By unspoken agreement they all got to their feet. As people disappeared up the stairs and out the front door, Adam went into the study and took an envelope from a box, then put the postcard inside. He tucked it into his shirt pocket.

He spun when he heard a noise behind him. Echo stood just inside the doorway.

He strode over to her without hesitation. He was dying to get out of this house and he wanted her to go with him. "Come to my house for what little remains of the night," he said against her hair. "I know it smells pretty bad, but upstairs I can open the windows and breeze from the lake—"

"I can't."

He waited for an explanation although heaven knew she didn't owe him one.

"I'm going to go pack," she added at last.

"But—"

She drew back, hands clutching his arms, fingers dangerously close to the bandage under his shirt and the torn flesh it protected. Her eyes glistened in the subdued light as she studied his face. "My stepfather just gave me the same lecture you gave me earlier tonight. He's adamant I leave immediately."

Adam didn't trust himself to speak.

"You don't want me here and neither does he. If the sheriff will let me, I'll catch a plane later today."

He stared at her for a second, then nodded slightly. "Just as well. I have to load up the ATV and go out to mend fences in the morning."

She dropped her hands and turned away. He heard her footsteps race up the stairs.

He ached to stop her, to tell her that she was wrong, he did need her.

Like his father had needed his mother.

Like Cody needed Cassie.

He would not go down that same path. His head knew better. But no way was he returning to his own house unarmed, not after tonight. He retrieved a handgun from the office cabinet, stuffed it in the waist of his jeans and took himself to his lonely bed.

THE NEXT MORNING, ECHO DRESSED for the plane again, but this time in different clothes. The other items, stained with blood and with memories she couldn't bear, had been discarded days before.

She knew from Pauline that all the men had left for the fields as soon as the sun came up. She suspected they were anxious to put a barrier between themselves and the horrors of the cave. That barrier was ranch work.

For the first time in her life she felt adrift, alone, like an outsider. Even the way Pete had chosen to move back here after Echo's mother died underscored the feeling that the years of her family life had been nothing but an interlude for him, an exile she didn't understand. Now that he was free to do as he pleased, he'd come home.

To his real family.

Home.

And then there was Adam. Don't forget Adam.

Impossible. She would never forget him. Never. And wasn't that a nice parting gift? A big old hole in her heart.

"If you're ready, I'll take your bag," her stepfather called from the open door.

"I thought Pauline was driving me to the fields," she said.

"I wanted a chance to say goodbye," he told her. He met her gaze briefly and Uncle Birch's comment from the night before rang in her ears. *You were in love with her too, Pete,* he'd said, and her stepfather had looked away.

Had her mother known?

"What time does your plane leave?" he added.

"Late afternoon."

"I'm glad you're getting out of here now. Things are bound to get ugly. And you have a great new job to look forward to."

Since when did he view her new job and move across country as a good thing?

After saying her farewells to Pauline, they drove out to the fields. Pete parked beside Adam's truck, which now had a dusty ATV roped into the bed, and insisted on transferring her belongings.

Echo paused before stepping down from the high platform of the diesel truck's frame, shading her eyes with her hand and looking out over the field. The mower was advancing toward them, Adam behind the wheel.

Giving into a whim, she jumped to the ground. The sprint across the freshly mown grass released some of the tightly wound springs in her body as well as her mind, and the payoff was the smile she saw on Adam's face as she looked up at him.

He put the tractor into Neutral. She climbed aboard and lacking a real place to sit, landed on his lap. He seemed surprised, and that made her laugh. "I didn't want to leave things the way they were," she told him truthfully.

"Aren't we driving into town together?"

"Yeah. I just wanted to say goodbye out here in the sunshine, before we see the sheriff and get all bogged down. We had some really nice times in with all the other stuff. I'll never forget them."

"I won't, either," he said.

"I'm sorry I didn't go home with you last night," she added with a swift glance up through her lashes. Yikes, that was kind of honest and out there.

He put the tractor back into gear and continued traveling toward the trucks. Echo looked ahead to gauge how much time they had. Her stepfather was loading her purse and laptop into the cab of the truck.

"It was the right decision," he said. "Truth is, my bed would seem mighty empty tonight if you'd been in it with me last night."

Their eyes met for a second. He closed the short distance between them and kissed her quickly. She'd been determined to confess about the concho. Even now it was in her pocket. But once again she shied away. What did it matter now and how could she ever explain to any of them her impulse to take it away?

In the next instant, they were at the truck. Her stepfather nodded at Adam as he offered Echo a hand down. Gesturing at the ATV he said, "Did you get the north fence, too?"

"Just the one up at the Hayfork field. I'll catch the other tomorrow morning."

Life would continue, that was the takeaway message Echo got from the exchange. Mowing would end, gathering and baling would commence, the herd would be driven home, fences would be mended—work would continue, the ranch would endure.

Pete gave Echo a rigid goodbye hug and made her promise to call. Before she even had her seat belt fastened, Pete Westin had taken Adam's place on the tractor. She watched his retreat with a heavy heart.

The drive into Woodwind was the beginning of the real goodbye, and before that, there was a session with the sheriff to get through. The envelope on the dashboard in front of Adam brought it all home. It must hold Aunt Melissa's last postcard.

Maybe she would give the concho to the sheriff, skip Adam altogether. Maybe Inkwell would agree to tell Adam his men had found it. Sure. A policeman lying to cover her sorry ass. That was going to happen....

"I'm kind of dreading this meeting with Sheriff Inkwell," she admitted.

"It's just to sign statements about the day Willet died and probably give a formal one about last night with the Garvey boys."

"Are you forgetting about your mother?" she asked.

"Of course not."

"Maybe the sheriff will have heard if it was really her down in that cave."

He pulled to a stop in the parking lot near the courthouse. Turning in his seat, he took both her hands in his. "Of course it's Mom, who else?"

"Then who murdered her, Adam?"

"Not my father," he said adamantly.

"I agree." She focused for a second on the new grass stain she'd acquired in her crazy dash across the field and for just a second, the memory of Adam's lips on hers and his arm wrapped around her brought a wave of need she had to fight off like an attack of wasps. "I watched your father last night," she continued, making herself stay on track. "He was beyond broken. I can't imagine him killing Aunt Melissa." Or anyone else, she decided. "Who killed her, Adam?"

"Maybe the guy down there with her. Maybe he pushed her into that crevasse and then shot himself in the head and fell. Or maybe she killed him and then herself although it's really hard to picture the mother I barely remember shooting someone right in the middle of his forehead."

"You realize if anything you just said is true it still leaves the question of who sent the postcard?"

"Yeah, I do."

"I'm just wondering what good the postcard can be after all these years. Everyone in your family must have touched it at one time or another."

"Who knows. Handwriting analysis or something. We'll let Inkwell worry about that. He's not quite the folksy incompetent he pretends to be."

As she shoved her hand in her pocket, her fingers grazed the metal of the concho.

Adam grabbed the envelope from the dashboard and opened it. He looked up and met Echo's gaze. Then he turned the envelope upside down.

It was empty.

Chapter Sixteen

Echo waited in the truck while Adam went inside for his doctor appointment. It took much longer than either of them had anticipated and she was nervous as she sat there waiting for him.

When Adam finally arrived he carried a handful of papers in his hand.

"Everything okay?" she asked.

"Besides it taking forever, yeah." He leaned across the seat and stuffed the papers into the glove box. "Some poor old guy had a heart attack right there in the office."

"That explains the siren I heard about an hour ago."

He nodded as he started the truck. "Still adamant about not catching your plane?"

"Yes. You'll have to put up with me a little longer. This postcard business changes things."

"It was never a matter of putting up with you, Echo."

She smiled at that. "You said the envelope was in your truck all night?"

"I stuck it on the dashboard when I got back to the house so I wouldn't forget it this morning. Considering the unannounced guests I had earlier in the night, I decided to lock the truck. This morning I got up before daybreak, loaded the ATV, drove out to the Hayfork field and did my thing, loaded up again and drove back to the tractor to start mowing. The only one who went near the truck was Uncle Pete."

"Someone could have gone inside your house and taken the keys and followed you up to the Hayfork field. I assume it wasn't a secret you were going there."

"No, it wasn't a secret. Everyone knew. But I had the truck keys in my pocket. I lost the spare about two months ago. Keep meaning to make a copy. It had to be Uncle Pete."

"He must have known we'd suspect him."

"Which meant he saw an opportunity and grabbed it. Which means it was really important to him that the sheriff not see the card. Which means—well, what, exactly?"

"That's what we have to ask him. And that's why I have to stay. You didn't mention it to the sheriff?"

"Hell, no."

"Good."

They both fell silent. What was Pete thinking? Had he had something to do with Melissa Westin's death?

Not that they knew for sure it was her. The sheriff hadn't heard back yet though he'd promised to let them all know as soon as he had. He'd asked her to read her statement and sign it, asked Echo a few questions, told her she could leave. Adam said his meeting with Inkwell had been much the same.

The damn concho was still in her pocket.

They passed a long white car soon after they entered Open Sky land. Echo strained to see who was driving but couldn't make out a face through the tinted windows.

"That's Lonnie's car," Adam said. "I guess he finally got a chance to talk to Dad." Soon after that, they came to the field that had been mown that day. The machines were all parked along the fence. The vehicles that had carried everyone to the field that morning were gone.

Echo glanced over at Adam as he hit every pothole in his haste to find out what had called everyone from the field when there were still hours of daylight left.

As if they couldn't guess.

They'd soon know about Aunt Melissa. Echo could feel it in her bones. And knowing, they would be left to sort out who did what to whom all those years ago.

EVERYONE WAS STANDING AROUND in the front yard amid what seemed a sea of trucks. It wasn't just his family and Pauline who were present, but also Del Halverson and J. D. Oakes who had no doubt showed up to lend moral support. Del was ruddier than ever, his cheeks glistening with sweat as the sunlight caught him on the face. J.D. nursed a cigarette, tapping the ashes on the fender of a truck every once in a while. Jamie and Mike stood off to the side, eyes shaded by their hats.

Sheriff Inkwell's car was parked by the barn and as Adam slowed down, he saw the sheriff make his way through the gathering and climb into the open bed of one of the ranch trucks. Cody's dog, Bonnie, jumped up with him. The sheriff stood with his hands on his waist, staring out at everyone.

Echo had her door open before the truck had stopped moving and Adam followed quickly.

He immediately looked around for his Uncle Pete and found him standing next to Adam's father with J. D. Oakes on his other side. His uncle met his gaze for a second before looking away anxiously.

"Glad you made it," the sheriff called to Adam. He narrowed his eyes and stared at Echo. "I thought you were headed back to California, Ms. De Gris."

"I changed my mind," she said. "I can't leave until I know what's going on."

"Stop the chitchat, Clayton," Birch called. "Did you find out if it's Melissa?"

Beside him, J.D. patted his arm. "You know the sheriff, Birch. He'll get there in his own time. Be patient."

"I've been patient for too many years," he said.

Inkwell made a point of making eye contact. "Are you sure you want to discuss this out here in front of everyone?"

"Hell, yes. These are my friends and family. Most of them knew Melissa."

"Well then, I won't make this any harder on you folks than it already is. It's her, all right. The dentist is positive. And we might as well get this part over with, too. There was a second bullet down there and indications it passed through Melissa's rib cage and spine. We'll know more when there's a full examination of the remains. We're calling in a forensic anthropologist."

A collective hush swept through the crowd.

Adam met Cody's gaze. His face looked about the same as always, but the expression in his eyes was different and when he looked from Adam to their father, the distrust that blazed in them stunned Adam. And then it was gone and it might have been a trick of light or Adam's imagination.

As for their father? He looked like a man who had been told he had a week to live.

Echo's fingers slid against Adam's. He didn't dare meet her gaze.

One worry was over. His mother wouldn't have shot herself through the ribs if her intent was her own death which meant she was murdered. Somehow that was better than finding out she was a killer.

Had she been running away or coming back? Had she gotten as far as Canada before returning only to meet her death? Adam looked at his uncle again. He had to know why Pete had stolen that card.

The sheriff was speaking again.

"I can't tell you all how sorry I am. I knew Melissa, too. Not well, but she was a hard woman to miss. There's more you need to know, though, such as the identity of the man down in that crevasse with her."

"David Lassiter," Adam whispered to himself.

"His name was Edwin Day."

The silence this time was complete until Adam's dad tore his hat off his head. "Who in the dickens is Edwin Day?"

The sheriff consulted a small notebook he took from his shirt pocket. "Edwin Day, born in 1956, a native of Hamlin, Montana." He looked up as he added, "Mr. Day was an only child of an only child, no sisters, no brothers, no aunts or uncles or cousins. In fact, he was raised on his elderly grandparents' farm when his parents died prematurely in a car crash. At the time of his death, he was about as alone in the world as a man can get."

"Then what the hell was he doing in our cave?" Birch demanded.

"We don't know that. Right now it appears Mr. Day was shot in the head and his body was thrown into the crevasse where it landed on that ledge. After a while, nature took its course. Eventually, a tremor of some kind rattled the bones enough that most of the skeleton fell to the bottom. Our resident archaeologist says it appears Melissa's remains were already down there because her bones were found beneath his. Preliminary study of the skeletal remains indicate that both individuals died around the same time.

"Today my team scoured the bottom of the crevasse. In with a few ancient remains and some rotting cloth and shoes of a more recent nature, they found one more bullet, same caliber as the one we found in the skull. And they uncovered an old wallet. The leather isn't much good, but some of the items inside had been protected with a plastic coating including two driver's licenses. One was for Edward Day. The other was for David Lassiter. The photo on both pictures is of the same man. And there's no record of anyone named David Lassiter, but there was an Edwin Day who disappeared about the right time."

"Then this Day fellow signed on here using an alias?" Jamie said.

"Apparently."

"So what?" Birch said. "Lots of folks use a fake name when they're down on their luck. Rules weren't as tight back then as they are now. Lassiter or Day or whatever his name was knew his way around cows and could ride a horse. That was good enough for me." He looked around and focused on his pals. "He even helped you out before he came to work for me, didn't he, Del?"

"And J.D. before that," Del said. "Remember, J.D.? That first year or two you were here?"

"I remember," J.D. said. "And he worked for Lonnie before that. That was back before Lonnie lost his ranch in that card game."

The sheriff spread his hands as he focused a laserlike glare at Adam's dad. "I'm not worried about him using an alias to get a job, Birch. All I want to know is who shot him and Melissa and hid their bodies in *your* cave. That's all."

"We can't just ask Pete if he stole that postcard," Echo said when she and Adam finally found a place to talk without fear of being overheard.

"We have to," Adam said. They had walked to the lake

where Adam had pulled a small boat off the shore and rowed them more or less to the middle. A warm breeze stirred the water and Echo would have enjoyed the ambience if it wasn't for—well, just about everything.

As it was, sitting still proved to be something of a burden and being stuck in the bow with Adam's back to her was getting on her nerves.

"Anyway," he continued, "aren't you the one who said we had to talk to him?"

"That was before we knew for sure about your mother."

"What does that change?"

She didn't know how to explain it to him so he would understand. She wasn't even sure she understood. But she'd watched Pete today as the sheriff spoke. He'd looked as if he was a breath away from taking a nosedive into the gravel. She'd experienced a wave of unanticipated sympathy for him that surprised her in its intensity.

"Echo?"

"Pete and I were never really close," she began. She'd taken the concho from her pocket and rolled it now between her fingers as she spoke. "He was devoted to my mother. Her needs were so great, especially in the last few years, that he and I rarely interacted. I think he asked me to come on this trip with him because he wanted to find a way for us to be closer but he doesn't know how to do it. Frankly, I don't, either. If I start questioning him now about something this hideous, we'll never find a way. He's all I've got and I'm all he has left of my mother. Does that make sense?"

"Not if it means my father rots in jail for something he didn't do," Adam said, his voice very firm.

The concho caught the fading light. "If he killed her—"

"Wait, wait just a damn second." Adam turned partway on the seat and she closed her fingers around the metal disk. "Didn't you tell me that I needed to keep faith in him? Now that it might be your stepfather, you're ready to sell my dad down the creek?"

"He's your uncle," she pointed out.

"Yes, I know that."

Echo could not sit another moment. It was like fire ants raced in her veins. She popped to her feet. "Okay, I'll talk to Pete myself. Let's go."

"Sit down," he snapped as the boat rolled.

"No. I can't sit. I have to act. You're right. If Pete knows something we have to find out what, damn the consequences. Move over, I'll row."

"No, I'll row," he said as he plunged the oars into the water and took a herculean pull. Unfortunately, Echo was in the process of stepping onto the seat beside him. She scrambled for footing as the boat rushed forward. Arms waving, she toppled overboard with a splash. The momentum of her fall pushed the boat the opposite direction.

She came up at once, sputtering.

Adam sat several feet away, almost as wet as she was, staring at her. "Are you okay?"

"If I had a dollar for every time you've asked me that, I'd be rich," she spat.

"It's not my fault you're an accident looking for a place to happen." He started rowing toward her.

"Don't bother," she called. "I'll swim back to shore."

He stopped rowing, extended a hand. "Echo, come on."

"I'll swim. I could use the exercise."

He took a couple pulls away from her. Then he yelled, "Don't worry about the long, slippery green things in the water. Three-fanged lake snakes are said to be nonvenomous."

Echo looked into the deep, dark water, and then she smiled. The sudden dip had washed the fight right out of her. The concho was still in her hand. She paddled closer to the boat and this time accepted his help. He pulled her from the water though it took a little work on her part to struggle over the gunwale. She landed in the bottom of the boat like a fish.

He looked down at her. "I think we're on the same side. We should be trying to work together, not arguing."

"I agree, oh wise one," she said. She crawled up on the stern seat and plopped down facing him, pushing wet hair out of her eyes. "There are no such things as three-fanged lake snakes, are there?"

He leaned across the seat and whispered, "Nope," against her mouth before kissing her. His lips were warm and tasty, igniting a fire she knew there would be no opportunity to extinguish.

"I have to show you something," she said softly.

His smile faded at the ominous tone of her voice. She opened her hand to reveal the concho.

"Where did you get that?" he asked at last.

"Willet Garvey's house. And before you accuse me of being crazy, tell me something I don't know. I recognized what it was and where it came from almost at once. It was right by Willet's body. I knew I should leave it where it was, but considering his dying words, I knew I couldn't."

She stopped talking. He picked up the concho and closed it in his fist.

"He told me that he lost the hat sometime within the past few weeks. He can't remember when he had it last. He replaced it with a straw one for the summer."

"Why would Willet mention a hat as he lay dying?"

"He's not the only one who mentioned it. Hank Garvey did, too, the night he attacked us. He said his father knew it was a Westin because of the hat. A black hat they took to be mine. What if someone took Dad's hat and wore it out to Garvey's place?" He looked from the concho to Echo. "I don't know what this was doing in Garvey's house, I just know Dad didn't murder Willet."

"Adam, we have to prove your father is innocent. And mine, too."

"How do we do that?"

"I say we find out about Edwin Day. He has to be the key."

Adam pocketed the concho and picked up the oars. "What do you mean?"

"That dip in the lake woke up my brain. We've all been assuming your mother was killed because of some man and yet your father has been adamant all along that she liked to flirt but that's as far as it went. If he's right, then what was Edwin Day doing in that cave with her?"

"I'll tell you what Inkwell thinks. He thinks Mom and this guy were having an affair and that my father caught and killed them."

"You're right, he does."

"And I have to admit that it looks that way to me, too. Except for the postcard. Dad didn't leave the ranch after Mom disappeared. I remember that, so he couldn't have sent it. Maybe Mom went to Canada and then came home and was killed before she got to the house. Honestly, Echo, I don't know what to think or where to start."

"Your father said a cousin came by a few months after Day vanished. But the sheriff said Day was an orphan with no living relatives. So, who was *the cousin?*"

Adam nodded again, this time with some enthusiasm.

She didn't speak again until they rowed past the beached yellow shack that Adam had told her would be hauled onto the ice come winter. "When this is all behind us, will you take me ice fishing?"

His gaze settled on her. Maybe it was her imagination,

but she seemed to sense the same yearning for a future in his eyes that she felt growing in her gut. It would do neither of them any good, but try telling a heart it shouldn't feel what it feels.

"There's a history to that little building," he said. "I'll tell you if you come back."

Come back? Sometimes it seemed to Echo like she'd never get out alive.

Chapter Seventeen

They found Birch sitting alone on the porch steps, his head in his hands. It was a rare thing to see him like that, especially when there was still daylight, grass to be mowed.

He looked up as they approached. His expression didn't change.

As Echo excused herself to put on dry clothes, Adam sat down next to his father. "Where is everybody?"

"Cody took a call in the office. Pauline is cleaning her already clean kitchen and Pete went back to the cabin about an hour ago. Does it seem to you that he's been acting strange?"

"Everybody is under a lot of strain," Adam said evasively. "I have to ask you a question."

"I'm just about questioned out."

"This will be quick. Have you had any luck remembering the name of the man who came hunting for David Lassiter aka Edwin Day after he disappeared?"

Birch shook his head. "The sheriff asked me the same thing. I'll tell you what I told him. I think it had *Rock* in it. Like Rockwell or Rockhill or something."

"Can you remember anything else?"

"Let's see. Me and Lonnie were treating calves for scour, so that means it was late winter, early spring. Said he was vacationing nearby and just thought he'd stop by and see if I could help him figure out where his cousin went. That's about it."

"Lonnie Nielson was here at the ranch when this guy came by?" Adam asked, a glimmer of hope lighting a little corner of his heart.

"Yeah. It was back before he lost his big spread. We used to help each other out—oh, I get it. Maybe Lonnie would recall a name. It's possible."

"What did he want today?"

"I never talked to him."

"He was here. We saw him leaving."

"I know. He was at the house when we all came back, waiting for me I guess. But when he saw the sheriff, he took off without saying anything. I tried calling him a little while ago to ask him what's up, but he wasn't home."

"Call him again. Ask him about the cousin."

"As soon as Cody gets off the phone. Lonnie's number is in the office."

Adam got to his feet and offered his father a hand. "Dad, did you ever figure out what happened to your black hat with the concho band?"

Birch shook his head. "Pauline thinks I left it at Lonnie's house a few weeks ago. I'll ask him about that, too. Hate to lose that band. Your mother gave it to me. It's about all I have left of her."

Lonnie. Lonnie who was acting "squirrelly" and obsessing about Willet Garvey's death....

Cody was just hanging up the phone when they entered the office. His face was a mask. He jerked his head at Adam and the two brothers left their father to call Lonnie. What now?

"I have to leave," Cody said. Bonnie stood by his leg, gazing up at him, panting. His fingers grazed her head. The dog sensed something was up.

"Where?"

"I'm not saying. And before you ask, I don't know how long I'll be gone."

Adam focused more closely on his brother. "What's this about? Oh, no. Don't tell me you got a call from your detective."

Cody nodded.

"You can't leave now. Things are heating up—"

"I have to leave now. Tonight." He started toward the stairs.

"Cody, damn it, man, how can you go at a time like this?"

Cody turned to face Adam. His dark eyes burned. "Maybe if Dad had gone after Mom she'd still be alive. I'm not making the same mistake. This might be the last time I can get close to Cassie and I won't throw it away." In a flash, he was halfway up the stairs, passing Echo on her way down, Bonnie scrambling to keep up on the slick wood.

"Did your father remember the name of the supposed cousin?" she asked as she stopped in front of Adam.

Adam looked away from his brother's retreating figure. He finally managed to form a single word. "No."

"What's wrong?"

"Cody is leaving."

"Now?"

"He's got a lead on his wife."

She was silent a moment, then touched his face. He looked down at her. "I guess he feels like he has no choice," she said.

Her fingers felt like satin against his skin. He wanted to bury all his anxiety in her. He had no idea if that was even a right thing to want. "I guess."

His father appeared a moment later. "Lonnie still isn't

answering the phone. I'll try again in a little bit. He and Janine never stay out too late."

Adam suddenly understood why Echo had stood up in the boat and tried to climb over him to take the oars. The thought of sitting there waiting for the next ax to fall was too much. "Come on, Echo, we'll go on over to his place and catch him when he comes home."

ONCE AGAIN THEY DROVE IN silence. Echo wasn't sure what Adam was thinking. Her mind jumped between two things. One, Pete. Why had he taken the postcard? How deeply was he involved? Was it possible he'd killed Adam's mother and Edwin Day and then packed up his family and left Wyoming? Would anyone remember if he had traveled to Canada that year? Had he mailed that postcard to cover his own guilt?

Was her stepfather a murderer?

Was that the real reason she'd dragged her feet about questioning him? Face it. Even now, wasn't she glad to be driving out to talk to a man she'd never met so she wouldn't have to confront her stepfather?

When that train of thought became too uncomfortable, she snuck a glance at Adam and mused about the fate that had reintroduced them at this one miserable juncture of their lives. Her brain told her to be careful but her heart, headstrong as a willful two-year-old, said to hell with caution.

"Oh, man, I don't like the looks of that," Adam said, startling her. She looked through the windshield to see dark smoke hovering over the hillside ahead, smudging the evening air. In the next moment, an emergency truck raced past them going the other direction, siren blaring.

"There have to be a lot of houses out this way," Echo said, although the truth was it looked like the hill was actually a ritzy neighborhood with large plots of lands and few homes.

A fire truck passed them going slower, headed back to town. Adam sped up. "Lonnie and his wife live near the top of that hill," he said. He pulled through the gates after a series of switchbacks and slowed as two fire trucks and a half dozen firemen came into view.

What was left of what appeared to have been a huge house was a smoldering mass of burned lumber, the roof crashed into the middle. Some of the fireman still directed water at the site while others were in the process of rolling hoses. It looked as if a few neighbors were standing around, talking in hushed tones.

"The firemen are still wearing their turnout gear," Adam said as the truck came to a stop. "It must have just happened." He gestured at the long white car parked next to a detached garage. "It looks like they were home."

A tall, lanky man dressed in a short-sleeved Western shirt approached the truck. An expensive-looking camera hung around his neck. "Do you know these folks?" he asked as Adam rolled down the window. The acrid smell of fire swept through the cab and stung Echo's eyes.

"They're family friends. I see their car over there. Are they okay?"

The man looked toward the house, then back. "Some of the neighbors got over here in time to help the husband get the woman out of the house. They took her off in an ambulance. The man went with her. He was staggering and coughing but at least he was walking under his own steam."

"Who are you?" Adam asked but he could have just asked her. Echo recognized a journalist a mile away.

"Reporter with the *Tribune*. I caught the 9-1-1 on my

CB and got over here soon after the first trucks. What can you tell me about these folks? What's your name?"

The sound of a siren racing up the hill caught everyone's attention. Echo looked through the back window. She could see a flashing red light but little else thanks to the ATV still strapped in the truck bed being in the way. In her sideview mirror, she watched the sheriff get out of his official white SUV.

The reporter immediately veered away to intercept him, but Inkwell waved him off as he marched determinedly to Adam's window. "What are you doing out here?"

Adam explained. Echo noticed he didn't say a word about coming to find the alleged cousin's name. He finished with a question of his own. "Are Lonnie and Janine okay?"

The sheriff stared at him for a few seconds. "The wife was apparently napping down in the basement and that's where the fire started. She's in bad shape. Lonnie was upstairs. He seems to have been asleep, as well."

"How did it start?"

"That's for the fire marshal to determine."

"We'll head over to the hospital and see if we can help Lonnie," Adam said.

Inkwell lowered his voice and checked to see if the reporter was still close by. "I suggest you go home. My deputies are over at your place right now collecting everything that shoots a .22 caliber bullet."

"What are you talking about?" Adam demanded. "Why?"

"Ballistics tests just came back on the bullet that killed Willet Garvey. By some miracle of timing that defies explanation, they also came back on the two bullets we found inside your cave."

A chill ran through Echo's entire body as the sheriff lowered his voice even more. "All three bullets were fired from the same gun," he added.

Beside her, Adam's knuckles turned white as he gripped the steering wheel.

"You might want to advise your father to call his attorney."

Chapter Eighteen

J. D. Oakes and Del Halverson were both at the ranch when Adam and Echo returned. Pete was conspicuously absent. The deputies were in the process of carting off the last of the weapons as per their warrant.

As soon as they'd driven away, it was up to Adam to explain what had happened at Lonnie's place. The news hit all of the older men hard.

"The fire started in the basement?" Del said. "Are you sure?"

"Positive," Adam answered.

His father immediately started making plans to collect Lonnie and bring him back to the ranch if the hospital would release him but of more interest to Adam was the meaningful glance J.D. and Del exchanged.

"Lonnie never got here today to talk to Dad," Adam said, leading the two of them aside as his father went into his office to exchange slippers for boots. "I get the feeling you guys know what he was worried about. The time for secrets is over."

"Your Dad is going to the hospital," Del said. "If Lonnie wants to talk, he'll talk."

"Hell, I'll talk," J.D. said. "I'm worried about Lonnie. From what Adam said, Janine could have died tonight, might still not make it. Lonnie will blame himself if he, well, you know."

"I don't know," Adam said as Echo joined them. "Tell me what you mean."

"Oh, hell," Del said with a sigh. His face, unnaturally pale for him, seemed to blanch even further as he added, "Lonnie had a collection down there in that basement."

"What kind of collection?" This from Echo.

"Artifacts from all over the place," Del said. "Janine didn't know anything about it. He showed us the stuff a few weeks ago, after a card game. Your dad wasn't coming to the games 'cause of that busted knee. Anyway, after Willet got himself killed, Lonnie confessed the last few things he bought came from Garvey. According to Lonnie, he didn't know Garvey stole them from your cave. He swears he wasn't in cahoots with Willet but he'd met with the man several times. He didn't know who had seen him at the Garvey place and if that someone might come forward after the murder."

J.D. shook his head. "If Lonnie panicked and decided to burn down his basement to get rid of the evidence, he never meant to hurt Janine. Sure he'd inherit all her money, but he'd be alone." He stroked his mustache and sighed. "He said guilt over buying stolen things from Garvey was eating him up. He wanted to confess it all to your father. But Lonnie isn't the bravest guy around."

Adam and Echo looked at one another. What did all this mean?

"We're going with your father to the hospital," J.D. added, slapping Adam on the arm. Unfortunately, he hit the wounded one and Adam had to stifle a grimace. "If Lonnie comes back here, be sure to keep an eye on him. If he started that fire, I wouldn't put it past him to do something else equally drastic."

Echo walked the two men to the door as Adam went into his father's office. To his absolute astonishment, the black Stetson sat on the desk.

"Hold down the fort, I'll be back soon," his dad said as he grabbed truck keys from the top of a bookcase.

Adam picked up the Stetson. "Wait a second, Dad. Where did your hat come from?"

"I found it behind the gun case when I was unlocking it for those damn deputies. It's missing a concho. I suspect your brother's dog had a go at it. Pauline said she'd keep an eye out for it. I have to run."

"Wait. Did the deputies go over to my place and get the Smith & Wesson?"

"I didn't know you had it. I think their warrant just covered my property. You own the land your house sits on."

"But the gun is registered to you. I took it over there after that little visit from the Garvey boys. You better call the sheriff in the morning and tell him about it."

There was a soft knock on the open door frame and they both turned to see J.D. "You coming, Birch?"

"Yeah. I'm coming."

Adam took the hat with him when he returned to the living room. Echo had plopped down in front of the empty fireplace. She was thumbing through the cigar box, pausing to peruse each photo. Her eyebrows lifted when she saw what he carried.

"Is that your father's?"

"Yep. He found it tonight on the floor behind the gun case. One of the conchos is missing."

"The hat couldn't have been there long or Pauline would have come across it before now," Echo said.

"The general consensus is Bonnie chewed on the band. Does it look chewed on to you?"

"No," Echo said as the dog who leaned against her leg managed to look offended by the suggestion. Echo tousled her gold ears. "And unless she's learned to drive and open doors, how did she deposit one of the missing conchos inside Willet Garvey's house?"

"Echo, if you hadn't taken that concho, the police would have picked it up. Tonight, when they searched for weapons, they would have found the hat with the missing concho and put two and two together."

"I hadn't thought of that. How did the hat end up here?"

"We never lock a door. During busy seasons, the house is often unattended for hours at a time."

"Meaning just about anyone could have returned it, but why?"

"To frame Dad for Willet's murder. Why else?"

"But why did someone even want to kill Willet?"

"It's got to be tied into the artifacts. Lonnie was buying them from Willet but he didn't know where Willet was getting them. When he figured it out, he panicked. The question is, did he panic before or after Willet was killed?"

"Everyone agrees the artifacts aren't really valuable monetarily. Plus, Willet died the day before the remains were discovered in the cave and yet the same gun killed the three people years apart. None of this makes sense, but I can feel a noose tightening around your father's neck."

"You watch," Adam said. "If ballistic tests show one of our guns fired those bullets and they get a new search warrant, the next thing we'll find is a bag of cocaine hidden away in Dad's desk."

They looked at each other for a heartbeat and then both rose at the same time. An hour later they'd searched the office. No drugs, but it was a huge ranch and evidence could be planted in a million different spots.

They sat back down on the sofa and Echo picked up the

box again while Adam studied the band. It did not look chewed to him....

"What's this?"

He shook himself out of his reverie and turned his attention to Echo as she lifted a tan business card from the cigar box. "It was stuck against the front wall. It's the same color as the box." She flipped it over in her hand. "'William Stonehill,'" she read. "Who's that?"

Adam took the card. "Never heard of him." One side was printed with the logo and information for a feed store in Woodwind that had gone out of business two decades before. The second side had William Stonehill written across it in pencil along with a phone number. "Area code 406," he read aloud. "Montana."

"Where in Montana? Can you tell?"

"No. The whole state has the same area code." He flipped the card. There was nothing on the other side. "It had to be in the box at least as long as the pictures, but who knows, it could have been in there for years before that." He flipped the card onto the tabletop. "Echo, where's Uncle Pete? Isn't it odd that he didn't come into the house during all this commotion?"

"Pauline said he didn't feel well."

"I think it's about time we got to the bottom of what he knows."

ECHO RAPPED HER KNUCKLES against the cabin door, waited a few seconds, then called out her stepfather's name. A faint "Come in" reached her ears. She and Adam walked directly into the living area, which wasn't all that big. Honey-gold knotty pine walls and antique braided rugs lent the place a cozy air that somehow didn't translate tonight.

The reason was the man sitting on a straight chair staring into a dark fireplace. Pete glanced up as though he'd been waiting for a firing squad. He looked ten years older than he had just three days before.

Echo crossed the room and knelt beside his chair. She had planned on questioning him gently, but the guilty look in his eyes unnerved her so that subtlety flew out the window. "Why did you take the postcard?"

"I didn't—"

"Yes, you did," she said. "Don't lie about it. We have to know why."

Pete shook his head. There were tears in his eyes. Echo's heart went out to her stepfather, but she resisted the urge to let him off the hook. She didn't believe for a moment that he would hurt anyone, but it was obvious he knew something.

"Echo has come very close to danger more than once and she might again," Adam said. "That's unacceptable to me. Isn't it to you?"

"Yes, but it doesn't make sense," he said quickly, glancing at Echo, and the tenderness she saw in his eyes communicated things he'd never been able to put into words. She gripped his hand. "Just tell us why you took it."

Pete's mouth opened and closed. He covered his face with his free hand, then lowered it. It took him sixty seconds before he finally spoke. "I thought the police might be able to tell that Melissa didn't really write the postcard. I couldn't take the chance."

Adam said, "Take what chance?"

The tears ran down his cheeks, following the grooves etched by time. "I was trying to protect my brother."

Echo immediately looked up at Adam who stood so still she could see his heartbeat in his throat. "Dad sent the postcard? How—"

"No, I sent it." He transferred his gaze to Echo. "I'd

traveled to Ontario in the past and brought home a bunch of postcards only your mother knew about. When things started heating up for Birch, I copied an old card of Melissa's that was lying around, one she'd sent earlier that year when she was gone for a while. Then I put it in an envelope and sent it to a Canadian friend with directions to send it here as a kind of joke. Birch had to know she couldn't have sent it but you should have seen him showing it around. It gave me the chills."

"How could Dad have known she didn't send it?" Adam said. "What do you mean?"

"I had to protect Birch," Pete mumbled. He took a deep, shuddering breath and finally mumbled, "He killed Melissa."

Adam took a step back. "No."

"I knew it had to be one of those spontaneous things, you know, a crime of passion," Pete said, his voice rising. "I didn't know then he'd killed the cowpoke, too. I thought he had just lost his temper and went too far and your mother ended up dead and he hid her body. I had to get the law off his back. I had to save the ranch. I thought I could live with knowing, but, Echo, when your mother started asking questions about the postcard, thinking she recognized it from those in the drawer, I knew it was time to get you and her away from here."

His gaze swiveled back to Adam. "I worried every day of my life about leaving you boys, but I knew Birch would never hurt you. It was your mother who pushed his buttons. He loved her so much."

"Did you see him do it? How do you know he killed her?"

Pete shook his head. "I came into the house that night. They didn't know I was there. I heard the fight and it wasn't just a squabble, they were really going at it. Then

Melissa exploded out the back door and I stood there in the shadows trying to figure out what to do. That's when I saw Birch come out of the den toting that old .22 he's still got. He went after her. I followed him, then lost him out where we used to have a bunkhouse. I thought I heard a shot, but I wasn't sure, it wasn't loud, and I told myself someone was shooting coyotes."

"But that doesn't mean—"

"Next day Melissa was gone. I'm not sure when Lassiter disappeared. Birch waited a few days then called the cops. I was there when he told them his version of what happened. He never admitted anything about going after Melissa or taking a gun or nothing. He lied to them."

"What did he do when the postcard came?"

"Acted all happy. I kept thinking about that noise. I couldn't swear what it was. I checked out the bunkhouses and couldn't see anything wrong. But I knew I had to get Althea and Echo out of here. We couldn't stay. And now I wish I'd never come back." He looked into Echo's eyes. "It was selfish of me to bring you here after all those years of keeping you away. I wanted time with you. I never dreamed all this would happen—"

Echo ran a hand through her short hair. This was a nightmare. She looked up at Adam, who was standing there, shaking his head.

"No," he said. "I don't believe it. There has to be another explanation." He paused for a moment and that's when Echo heard a car outside. Adam apparently heard it, too. He crossed to the window and held open the drape for a second, then dropped it. "Dad and the others are back. Looks as though they brought Lonnie with them. Time for a chat."

"I can't bear to look him in the eye," Pete said.

"You don't have to," Adam said. "I'll do it for you."

Echo got to her feet. "And I'll help."

THEY FOUND J. D. OAKES smoking on the porch. "They're inside," he said as he snuffed out the cigarette. "I've had about as much of Lonnie as I can take. Tell Del I'm going to go over to say hello to Pete. He can come get me when he's ready to head home."

As Adam opened the front door, his father turned to face them, his eyes red and moist. Del and Pauline were in the process of helping Lonnie up the stairs. Lonnie was making a lot of noise, but none of it was intelligible. Birch took Echo by the arm and guided them both into the living room. He kept his voice soft. "Janine died," he said.

Echo gasped. "Oh, no."

"She didn't even make it to the hospital," he added. "They're doing an autopsy. There's some question whether the fire killed her or something else. Lonnie is a mess, hardly coherent. Del seems to be the only one who can handle him."

Things were spiraling out of control but Adam still couldn't see how it all connected. He needed to confront his father with what he'd just learned from his uncle, but now seemed like a terrible time to do it. Nevertheless, now was all they had. "I want to know why you never told anyone you went after Mom with a gun the night she ran out," Adam said.

The shocked hurt in his father's eyes almost knocked Adam off his feet. "Who told you—"

"Pete saw you," Echo said softly. "He was in the house and he saw you. He even followed you but he lost you and he thinks he heard a shot—"

"Now wait just a minute," Birch interrupted, the initial

shock shifting into anger. "Okay, I did go after her and I did take a rifle out of the gun case because the case wasn't locked and it was right there—we'd been having trouble with coyotes. I thought if Melissa wandered too far away she could be in trouble. Then I realized she wasn't that stupid so I came back into the house. I never fired the rifle."

"Was it a .22?"

"Hell, I don't remember."

"Why didn't you tell the police?"

"How would it have looked? Who sent that blasted postcard?"

"Uncle Pete," Adam said. "Trying to save you and the ranch."

His father swore.

Pauline appeared in the large open doorway, her face distraught. "You have to come help. Hurry. Lonnie stumbled."

Adam sprinted up the stairs, his father climbing more slowly behind him. They found Lonnie slumped against a chair in the hallway, Del holding on to one arm. They got him to his feet and onto the bed, but he'd gone all boneless and felt as heavy as a bag of wet sand. His face and hands were streaked with soot. Adam hated himself for thinking it but the thought crossed his mind that it was all an act, and overkill to boot. He told Del where he could find J.D., then left the others to help Lonnie.

When he returned to the living room he saw Echo had picked up the business card she'd found in the cigar box earlier that evening. A glance at the clock showed it was almost two o'clock in the morning. They should both sleep.

"Do you believe Dad?" Adam asked as he sat down next to her.

She nodded. "I believe both of them. Adam, remember you told me that your father said Edwin Day's cousin's name had the word *rock* in it. What if he remembered it wrong? What if it was really *stone*?"

Adam mentally kicked himself. What else had he missed? "What are the chances the phone is still connected?" he said as he punched in the number on the card.

It rang once, then switched to an answering machine, "You've reached the office of Mariket and Clarke. Please call back during regular business hours or leave a number and your call will be returned."

He hung up, and using the search engine in his phone, punched in *Mariket and Clarke, Montana*. "They're in Hamlin," he told Echo a moment later when the results filled the small display.

"Hamlin is where Edwin Day was from." She'd listened in on the recording and now studied the screen. "Look. Mariket and Clarke are attorneys."

"Yeah." He checked his watch. "Hamlin is four hours from here. If I leave now, I'll be there early tomorrow. I'll go tell Jamie. This is really going to leave him shorthanded, but I don't see an option. There has to be something we're missing."

"I'll go grab a few things," Echo said.

"I wish you'd—"

She held up a warning hand. "Of course you do. I know you can go alone. I'll be ready in five minutes."

"You're the most stubborn—"

But she was already gone.

Chapter Nineteen

It was Echo's intention to keep Adam company during the drive, but he didn't want to talk and she didn't blame him. She fell into an uneasy slumber, her head propped against her window. She awoke at sunrise, cramped, stiff and wooly mouthed.

Adam flashed her a glance. "Morning." He had one elbow outside his window, one hand on the steering wheel and he sounded wide awake. His hat was behind the seat, his short hair caught the breeze. She studied his profile for a moment. He looked incredibly handsome, sexy, exciting, different somehow than he had a few days earlier, as though the stress of the past few days had altered something in his face.

As though experience had carved away some of his youth.

"I was having a dream Lonnie was standing outside your house tossing flaming matches through a window," she told him when he caught her staring. She hugged herself against a sudden chill. "I don't think I've ever seen Lonnie before tonight, let alone met him."

"You need something hot in your stomach," Adam said. "There's a truck stop up ahead. Let's get something to eat and wait until Mariket and Clarke opens."

The truck stop appeared on the horizon and grew into

a sprawling building surrounded by huge parking lots filled with long-distance trucks. An hour later, face and teeth scrubbed, stomach full of coffee and an omelet, Echo climbed back into Adam's truck.

Hamlin was a bigger town than Woodwind, but not by much, and there was little traffic at this time of day. Thanks to the GPS, they found the office easily and parked on the street out in front. Adam's truck, plastered with ranch dirt and grass debris, the equally disreputable ATV still anchored in the bed, looked out of place parked next to the stately old buildings.

The room they entered was barren except for a couple tall ladders pushed against bare walls and paint cans, rollers and brushes stacked in a corner. Paint-splattered tarps covered the floor. Swatches of different colors bisected walls as though a color palette was in the process of being worked out.

A little bell had tinkled over the door when they opened it. Within seconds, a middle-aged woman with short auburn hair walked through a connecting door. She stopped when she saw them. "I was expecting the painters." She checked her watch. "They're late as usual. May I help you?"

"We're looking for a man named William Stonehill," Adam said. "Does he work here?"

"No," she said, taking off a pair of reading glasses and letting them dangle from a beaded cord around her neck. "I'm the only one who works here now." She put out a hand. "My name is Amanda Clarke."

Echo swallowed her disappointment. Of course it couldn't be that easy. "What happened to Mariket?" she asked, shaking Amanda's hand.

"Divorce, hence the remodeling. Even his name will be

gone as soon as the glass guy gets around to scratching it off the window. Hallelujah. Now what can I do for you?"

"And you don't know anyone name William Stonehill?" Adam said.

"Now, I didn't say that." She looked them both over and added, "Why do you want him?"

"We're trying to track down anything we can about another man by the name of Edwin Day," Echo said.

Amanda gestured at the room she'd just left. "Come have a seat." They followed her into a slightly larger office with warm yellow walls and high windows. A vase of sunflowers sat on a shelf. She pointed out a pair of matching chairs for them and seated herself behind the desk, folding her hands in front of her. "I haven't heard Ed's name in a long time. May I ask how you know him?"

"We don't," Adam admitted. "His bones turned up in a cave on my family's property. He's been dead a long time. How is his name familiar to you?"

A fleeting smile curved her lips. "William Stonehill is my father. My name is Clarke thanks to my first marriage. Anyway, Dad is in a memory care place now. Most days, he doesn't know who I am. He doesn't talk at all anymore, but once in awhile, the expression in his eyes makes me think he still recognizes me. I treasure those times."

"And Edwin Day?"

"An enigma. I'm sorry, I can see that I'm confusing you. Edwin Day was a friend of my father's. They were really different. Dad was an attorney. In fact, this was his office back then. He was the salt-of-the-earth type, you know, dependable and honest as the day is long. Ed was about as opposite from that as a man could get. He'd been raised by his grandparents and when they died and he was free to cut loose, he really cut loose. I think he was married like four times. Always running around with someone new. But he and dad both liked to go fly fishing and sometimes friendships just kind of defy logic.

"Anyway, when I was about fifteen or sixteen years old, Dad hired Ed, who had just gotten another divorce, to do some undercover work for a family back east who had contacted Dad for help. Strictly under-the-table and hush-hush."

Adam held up a hand. "Undercover work. Wait, are you saying Ed Day did undercover work in Wyoming, out near Woodwind?"

"I'm not sure exactly where. The Rocky Mountains somewhere."

"Which explains his other identity," Echo said. She leaned forward and explained. "He was found with two driver's licenses."

"Who or what was he investigating?" Adam asked.

"A guy by the name of Buzzby Crush, I kid you not. Crush was a hit man in Jersey way back when. The story went that he took a boatload of money for a multiple hit and then disappeared without fulfilling his contract. The mob was hell-bent on finding him but so was the family of an innocent girl who got caught in the cross fire of an earlier assassination. The investigation dead-ended in the Midwest. That's when the girl's family hired Dad. Eventually Dad uncovered rumors that suggested Crush had settled near a small town in western Wyoming so he hired Ed to go hang out and chat people up and see if he found anything."

"Good grief," Echo said.

"What did Buzzby Crush look like?" Adam asked.

Amanda Clarke sat back in her chair. "No one knows. He was very careful not to have his picture taken. Plus Dad said it was his M.O. to change his appearance for each client and each hit."

"Did Ed Day find any proof that this man was in Wood-wind?"

"I gather he called a few times and talked to Dad. Nothing definitive as I understand, but I also got the feeling he felt he was closing in. And then the calls stopped coming."

"Do you know how old Crush was?"

"When he disappeared? I don't remember. Not too old. As I recall, he came out of nowhere, built a reputation very quickly and then faded away with all that money. I think he was only in 'the business' for a couple years or so." She steepled her fingers. "Now it's my turn to ask a question. How did you run across my father's name?"

Adam took the card from his pocket and handed it to the older woman. "I think my father wrote it down after talking to your father about what happened to Edwin Day. He probably scribbled it on the first scrap of paper he found."

Amanda ran a finger over her father's name, a wistful smile curving her lips. "And you live in Woodwind, is that right?"

"Nearby, on a ranch."

"A ranch," she mused. "I'm remembering now. Dad took a fishing trip to Yellowstone several months after Ed disappeared. He stopped by the ranch where Ed was last known to be. He must have talked to your father. I gathered from my dad over the years that the local consensus had Ed running away with the rancher's wife. Oh dear, would that be your mother?"

Adam nodded.

"Dad told me years later that he hadn't found the story surprising given Ed's reputation with women, but he did wonder why any woman who had a family and a good life like she must have had would trade it for a life with Ed. He was highly undependable and it just struck Dad as odd that an educated woman like your mother would find that attractive. But you never know about people, do you?"

"As far as we know, they were friends and nothing more," Adam said. "You mentioned that Ed was getting closer to Crush. Why did your dad just let the investigation drop?"

"There was absolutely no proof of anything. After Ed took off, Dad decided Ed had been leading him on. See, Dad was sending Ed money after the calls. He figured Ed just wanted to keep the cash coming, so he reported progress, saying he was sure Crush was one of the ranchers he'd worked for and then moving on and claiming it was another one. Dad doubted any of the reports were true."

"Do you still have those reports?" Echo asked.

"Heavens no. That all happened a lifetime ago. It wasn't until years passed and Ed never showed up again that Dad began to wonder what had really happened to him and then his own problems with memory started. Now you say Ed was buried in a cave? What kind of accident—"

"He was murdered," Adam said. "Probably back before your father ever asked about him."

Her eyes widened. "Murdered? How?"

"A bullet through the forehead," he said quietly. "Execution style."

Echo clutched her stomach at the sound of the words, *execution style*. Could there really be any truth in this story? It seemed absurd and yet…

"My mother's skeleton was found in the cave with his," Adam added. "It appears she was shot, too, though not in the head. And now there's been another killing with the same weapon."

"Was the new victim killed execution style?"

"No, his murder was made to look like a drug deal gone wrong. But the man was digging around in the cave where the other two bodies were thrown."

"So he was a threat."

"Yes. I think so."

Amanda Clarke straightened up. "I sure wish I could be more help."

Adam rose to his feet. "You've given us a piece to the puzzle we didn't have before," he said, and extended his hand to Amanda. "Thank you. We'll see ourselves out."

Back in the first room, Adam ran a hand over his eyes. "How does this fit with Uncle Pete's and Dad's versions of that night?" he whispered.

"I don't know," Echo said.

"I keep thinking about Lonnie. I know what he told his friends, but think about it this way. Lonnie collects relics. Garvey comes up with something new only this time, Lonnie recognizes it because he last saw it years earlier when he hid two bodies. He decides to make sure so he stalks Garvey only he wears my Dad's hat to confuse the issue. When he finds out he's right, he kills Garvey with my dad's gun which he lifts from the house the same way he did before, leaves the concho at the murder scene and prepares for the fireworks. Then he starts the fire to get rid of the evidence."

"And his wife?"

Adam shrugged. "Maybe she was catching on. Maybe he wanted to get rid of her, too."

"Well, it all makes a kind of perverted sense."

"Yeah," he said, but then sighed. "But it could also be one of the others. They all lived away from Wyoming when they were young. They all came back after having done well. Del at the bank, J.D. with his mining operation and Lonnie when a great uncle died up in Canada and left him a small fortune. Even Uncle Pete was away. Dad is the only one who never left."

"It can't be Pete," she said, heart pounding, but of course, it could be. She knew he'd met her mother in New York, soon after Echo's birth. Her biological father had died before Echo was even born. After their whirlwind courtship, the new family had traveled to Wyoming. Later, Pete had moved them even farther west. At last Echo understood why he'd done that: he thought his brother was a murderer.

At least that's what he said. Everything he had told them was unsubstantiated.

Wait. He couldn't have killed Willet.

But he could have. He was out on a tractor with a truck at his disposal like everyone else, out of sight of the others for hours at a time, and most importantly, Willet had died the day after she and Pete had come back to Wyoming. No...

"We need to get back to the ranch," Adam said as they walked out on the sidewalk. "I'd call Inkwell if—"

"Not yet," Echo said. "Not until we run this by your dad."

"And Uncle Pete?"

"Your dad first," she said with a meaningful look. "He's the only one who never left Wyoming."

Chapter Twenty

She insisted on driving. He knew he was beyond exhausted, so he settled for calling the ranch, unsure who exactly to warn about who. It was a hopeless quandary and in the end, immaterial as no one picked up the phone. He wasn't even sure what kind of message to leave. He closed his eyes and tried to shut off his thoughts.

The next thing he knew he was startled awake by a sharp cracking sound. His eyes flew open to find Echo struggling with the wheel while the truck swerved radically to the right. Adam's hands flew up in the air as the vehicle careened over the top of a rocky embankment and sped down to a creek twenty feet below. It all happened so fast there wasn't time to do anything but brace himself.

Within a few seconds, the truck ran into a line of trees and came to an abrupt and crashing halt.

Both airbags inflated with the impact, then instantly lost air. He looked over at Echo and she met his gaze, lips trembling. "Let's get out of here," he said, flicking her seat belt open, then his own.

They tumbled out their respective doors and ran around the back toward each other. They met near the tailgate.

"Are you okay?" Adam asked Echo as he took her shoulders in his hands. There were tears in her eyes and she was shaking, but she nodded.

"You're not supposed to ask me that, remember?" she said, trotting out a laugh that sounded more than a little hysterical.

"What happened? Did we hit something?"

"No. Someone shot at us! I saw a car parked on the other side of the bridge. Then something dark extended through the window and the next thing I knew, our windshield cracked."

Adam glanced at his watch and found he'd slept away the last four hours which meant they were damn near home. He took a good look around. "This appears to be Butcher Creek. We're ten or twelve miles away from the ranch." He started pulling her along the hillside, glancing back at his truck as he did so.

"I don't want to go up there," she said, tugging his hand. "What if whoever shot at us is waiting?"

"We have to get home, Echo. If the shooter wants us dead, all he has to do now is stand up there and pick us off. Since he isn't, I assume that means he thinks we're dead or injured and have to walk back to the ranch. God knows what he'll do while we're mucking around out here." He took out his cell phone and punched in the ranch. The phone switched to the answering machine after the first ring.

Adam swore as he pocketed the phone. "It'll take awhile to walk that distance but we have to try." He looked down the hill at his dead truck, and a smile split his lips. "I have an idea."

Echo turned and looked and a second later, it was obvious she'd connected the same dots.

The front of the truck was crunched, but the bed was intact and contained his trusty ATV. They ran back down the hill.

ECHO RETRIEVED THE RIFLE Adam carried in the rack of his truck while he hacked away at the ropes that held the ATV in place. It took longer than usual to get the machine out of the bed thanks to the position the truck had landed. There wasn't much she could do to help until it was time to position the metal runners. He added more fuel from a can he carried, and they were ready to go. Much to her relief, he didn't return to the main road.

Instead Adam followed the creek until he settled on a good place to cross. "It's half the distance if we stick to the countryside," he told her over his shoulder.

The rifle fit into a scabbard mounted on the side of the vehicle, but juggling her purse and a box of ammo while trying to stay seated still took most of Echo's concentration. Soon the land began to seem familiar. She finally realized they were coming in from the lakeside and would pass Adam's place before getting to the ranch house.

After a steep climb, Adam paused for a second and they took in the vista. The fields lay all around them, golden now in the summer heat. They could even see a tractor or two. The ranch house lay beyond. And Adam's house was relatively close by, the sun behind it giving the illusion of a fairy-tale castle perched on the edge of the glittering lake.

"There's a car down there," Adam said.

"Where?"

"On the road."

"Oh, I see. The gray one." Echo's heart fluttered in fear. "Adam, the car that shot at us was a light-colored SUV."

"Half the cars in this county fit that description." As they watched, the car came to the fork in the road and swerved right, toward Adam's house.

"Were you expecting anyone?" she asked him.

"No." They waited until the vehicle hit his long driveway where it slowed down. A plume of dust billowed behind as it moved along the road. The vehicle rolled through the grove of trees and around to the back near the kitchen entrance where it came to a stop. They could barely see the driver and passenger doors open and two men emerge.

"It's hard to tell with the sun in my eyes, but the one closest to us kind of looks like your father," Echo said. "Isn't that a limp?"

"I think so. And the other one looks like the sheriff. Thank God, our luck has finally changed." He grabbed her around the waist. "I'm going on alone. You'll be safe up here and I'll come back after I make sure no one else is with them."

"Here we go again," she said.

He pulled her against him and kissed her, his lips demanding, his fingers on her throat tender. There was a message in his kiss and she knew what it was. This was it. This was the crux of everything. "If it comes to protecting you or myself, I'll protect you every time," he said softly. "It's safer for both of us if I go on alone."

"Like you always do."

"I don't always—"

"You keep running away from me or trying to push me away. Okay, you win, I won't fight you anymore. But think about this while you go charging off by yourself. You don't have to run from a woman before she runs from you."

"That's ridiculous."

"Is it?" She brushed off her cheeks, annoyed to find her fingers trembling. "You've spent almost your entire life thinking your mother left you, that you weren't lovable enough to make her stay."

"But she didn't leave—"

"Exactly," Echo said. "But you don't believe it. Not really. And yet, Adam, who's the bigger fool? The person so set in his ways that he can't see into his own heart or the person who refuses to accept he's never going to change?"

She turned away. A moment later, when she heard the ATV move off down the hill, she pivoted around to watch. "Goodbye, Adam," she whispered.

THE PROFOUND RELIEF AT HAVING the two men he knew he could trust in the same place at the same time filled Adam with renewed hope.

As for Echo?

He'd think about her later. Right now he would focus on the job at hand. No more equivocating. Get all the lies and deceptions out in the open, figure out exactly who Buzzby Crush had transformed himself into thirty years ago.

He stopped the ATV by the gate and got off, bounding over the split-rail fence, anxious to talk to his dad. He couldn't see the sheriff's rig from this side of the house, but he was sure he would have noticed if they'd left. He made his way directly down the path to the front door which he noticed was closed with the screen just as he'd left it the last time he was home.

Voices drifted through the door. His father's, then another, but it wasn't the easy drawl of the sheriff. Adam hopped up on the first step and glanced through the big front window. What he saw immediately drove him to the deck of the porch, hoping he hadn't been seen.

In that microsecond, the image of his father down on his knees with his hands behind his neck had burned itself into Adam's brain. And standing over him, the Smith & Wesson clutched in one hand, J. D. Oakes, a burning cigarette dangling from his lower lip.

Oakes.

And Adam had left the damn rifle on the ATV.

He quickly inched his way across the porch until he was able to see through the lower portion of the screen door. Their voices had been obscured by the roaring in his head, but now he fought that as he took in additional details: the tip of the barrel—the Smith & Wesson—pressed with Oakes's left hand against his father's right temple. The kerosene lantern Adam kept on the mantle clutched in Oakes's night hand. Oakes's voice, calm, reasonable. "—and so it's the end of the line, old buddy."

"You won't get away with it," his father warned.

"I'll get away long enough to disappear and reinvent myself again," Oakes said. "While the sheriff investigates your apparent suicide—using the same gun you used to kill Melissa, the detective, and Willet Garvey—I'll be liquidating my assets. All I need to do now is confuse the crime scene investigators for a while, and that's as easy as one, two, three."

With that, he flung the lantern against the hearth where it crashed, spraying kerosene across the floor and up the nearby wall. "One," he said, his voice cold now. Next he flicked his lit cigarette into the fuel and muttered, "Two," as flames erupted into life and immediately caught the edge of a curtain.

Adam knew what would happen with *three*. He stood up, stepped back and threw himself at the screen. It flew off its hinges as he crashed into the house.

J.D. spun around to stare at him, eyes wide in surprise. The gun swiveled with him. In the next instant, J.D. fired and Adam dropped to the floor, partly because he'd been hit and partly to make himself a smaller target.

He looked up immediately to find his father had used the opportunity to wrap his arms around J.D.'s legs and bring him down. The Smith & Wesson had slid away from both men and they were scrambling to get to it. J.D. had the edge. Adam was too far away to help.

And then someone leaped over the screen and streaked past him. Echo. Echo was there, running across the room, gasping for breath. She grabbed the gun a split second before J.D.'s fingers closed around the grip. As the older man reached up to grab it from her, she pointed it at him and fired.

J. D. Oakes screamed bloody murder.

Epilogue

"So, you're that irritating little girl who used to hog the top bunk at the hunting lodge?" Pierce Westin said.

He had arrived home a short while before, fresh off a private jet that had originated in Chatioux. He'd debarked wearing a tailored suit in which he'd made quite a dashing impression, but had since changed into jeans and boots. He looked totally at home standing around the center island in the ranch kitchen. You could take the Westin out of Wyoming, but you couldn't take the Wyoming out of a Westin.

"I had to hold my own against you guys," she said, sparing Adam a glance. "It was a struggle."

The doctors had operated on Adam's shoulder—the same one as before. He was expected to make a complete recovery but for now, he'd earned himself a sling. And thanks to the fire damage in his house, he'd had to move back to the ranch until he could fix it.

"I'm sorry you're going to miss meeting Analise," Pierce continued, shoving one of the red mugs across the counter for a refill. Echo was happy to comply. "You will come back for the wedding, won't you?"

"I'll be starting a new job," she said evasively. "But I'll try."

"She'll come back," Uncle Birch said with an affectionate smile. "She saved our lives. That means she's responsible for us now. Isn't that the way it goes, sweetheart?"

She laughed for the first time in two days or two weeks—hard to remember when something had seemed funny.

Birch Westin shook his graying head. "Who in the world would have thought old J. D. Oakes was really a mob hit man named Buzzy Crush? I looked him up on the Internet—it's suspected he has killed over two dozen people. Once he recovers from Echo's handiwork, he'll spend the rest of his life shuffling between courthouses and prison cells. I still can't believe it."

"He drugged Lonnie?" This from Pierce who was playing catch-up.

"Him and Janine both. Lonnie is still unclear on what happened, but one of his neighbors said they saw J.D.'s car at Lonnie's place right before the fire. The sheriff found a bottle of wine in Lonnie's house with J.D.'s fingerprints on it and traces of drug-laced wine inside. I guess he figured the bottle would be destroyed in the fire. He must have gone over there right after the sheriff told us about David Lassiter's real identity."

Pierce shook his head.

Echo might have shot Crush in the leg, but it hadn't hurt his vocal cords and he was willing to talk, apparently in the hope it helped his case. The night of Melissa Westin's and Ed Day's murders, Oaks had picked the lock on the Westin gun case and stolen the Smith & Wesson. He'd been spreading rumors about Melissa's supposed romance ever since he got wind that Ed Day was more than he seemed to be and had used a Westin gun to throw suspicion on Birch. He'd shot Ed, but then Melissa walked in on the murder so he'd killed her, too. He'd heard Birch talk about the cave and the fact that Melissa was the only one who went there so he chose that cavern to hide their bodies. He had replaced the gun the next day; no one knew it had ever been missing.

He stole the same gun when he saw Lonnie's collection and recognized a gold-headed relic as one he'd seen before. He had swiped Birch's hat and had planted the drugs and the concho, and he'd admitted the rest of the drugs were hidden out in the Westin barn, waiting to be "discovered," thanks to an anonymous tip. On the day he shot out the window of Adam's truck, he'd followed them to Hamlin. As soon as he had figured out what they were up to, he'd raced back to Wyoming and waited for them to show up so he could buy himself some time. After the truck had careened down the hill, he'd conned Birch by saying Adam had asked him to go get his father and retrieve the Smith & Wesson for the sheriff, then had turned the weapon on Birch in hopes of making it look like a suicide in a last-ditch effort to cover his crimes.

He'd been welcome in their home for over thirty years and he used much of that time lately to listen in on conversations and arrange false evidence.

Pierce glanced at the wall clock then at his father. "Echo's plane leaves in a few hours. Let's go find Uncle Pete and see if he's ready to give her a ride," Pierce said, clapping his father on the back. "I still want to know where in the heck Cody went. This is the second time he's taken off like this, you know."

It was on the tip of Echo's tongue to say she could find Pete herself, but Adam sent his family on their way. Once they were alone, he took her hand and cleared his throat. "You've been avoiding me."

She leaned against the counter and looked at their linked fingers.

"I know you hate for me to ask this, but are you okay?"

"Why wouldn't I be okay?"

"You shot a man."

"He was going to kill you."

"About that," he said, gripping her hand a little tighter. "How in the world did you get down the hill so fast?"

"I ran like hell."

"Did you see something that alerted you?"

"I had forgotten to give you the box of ammo and I thought you might need it."

"Ah. So you raced down there to give me the ammo."

"That's right. And when I got close enough, I saw you crash through the door so I—"

"—crashed right in after me without even stopping to consider what you might be getting yourself in for."

She shook her head. "Stupid, huh?"

He looked into her eyes, his gaze unflinching. "I'm afraid you're going to have to stay in Wyoming with me. You're just too reckless to be out on your own."

Tears bit the back of her nose at the suggestion his words posed. "You're the one in a sling," she said gently as she withdrew her hand. She'd tucked away the dreams of a future with him, folding them like one would a mourning gown, not wanting to damage it but unable to bear seeing it all the time.

His fingers caressed her cheek. "You have everything in the world waiting for you in New York," he said softly. "There's only one thing in Wyoming I can offer you and that's myself."

She met his gaze again, hers narrowed. "But—"

"Because I've been doing some thinking about what you said up on the hill. You were right. I was sure I could never be enough for you. I was afraid to even dream you could settle for me. If I've been stuck in my past since I was a little kid, it's about time I make some changes, isn't it?"

Echo allowed herself to melt a little. Just a little because did he mean all this?

"When you ran down the hill, Echo, you were more brave than anyone I could have imagined and you did it not out of fear but because you love me. I saw your face after you shot Buzzby. Admit it. You love me."

She leaned close and brushed her lips against his. "I admit it. I love you. Happy?"

"Yeah," he whispered, stroking her cheek with the backs of his fingers. Then he claimed her lips again.

"I'm the only man for you," he said softly when they came up for air. "You know it's true. We were made for each other."

Her heart thrashed in her chest like a trapped bird trying to beat down the bars of its cage. Could this be happening? Was it real? She touched his lips with her fingers. They were trembling again, this time with hope instead of despair. "Will you teach me how to drive a tractor and pull a calf and take me dancing and keep me amused on long winter nights?" she whispered. "Can you do all that?"

He stared deep into her eyes with such desire it stole her breath away. "Yes. Especially the last." And proved it by pulling her tightly in a one-armed embrace.

"I want *you* forever," he said against her hair, his voice

fierce. "I love you, Echo De Gris, and I'll give you the world if you can find a way to love me back."

She pulled away and looked up at him. The cage was open, her heart was free. "Silly man. Don't you know you *are* the world?"

* * * * *

Don't miss the gripping conclusion of
OPEN SKY RANCH *by Alice Sharpe*
in November 2011.
Will Cody Westin finally learn the truth
behind his wife's disappearance?
Look for WESTIN FAMILY TIES
wherever Harlequin books are sold!

COMING NEXT MONTH

Available November 8, 2011

You can find more information on upcoming
Harlequin® titles, free excerpts and more at
www.HarlequinInsideRomance.com.

HICNM1011

REQUEST YOUR FREE BOOKS!
2 FREE NOVELS PLUS 2 FREE GIFTS!

♦ Harlequin®
INTRIGUE™
BREATHTAKING ROMANTIC SUSPENSE

YES! Please send me 2 FREE Harlequin Intrigue® novels and my 2 FREE gifts (gifts are worth about $10). After receiving them, if I don't wish to receive any more books, I can return the shipping statement marked "cancel." If I don't cancel, I will receive 6 brand-new novels every month and be billed just $4.49 per book in the U.S. or $5.24 per book in Canada. That's a saving of at least 14% off the cover price! It's quite a bargain! Shipping and handling is just 50¢ per book in the U.S. and 75¢ per book in Canada.* I understand that accepting the 2 free books and gifts places me under no obligation to buy anything. I can always return a shipment and cancel at any time. Even if I never buy another book, the two free books and gifts are mine to keep forever.

182/382 HDN FEQ2

Name	(PLEASE PRINT)
Address	Apt. #
City	State/Prov.	Zip/Postal Code

Signature (if under 18, a parent or guardian must sign)

Mail to the **Reader Service:**
IN U.S.A.: P.O. Box 1867, Buffalo, NY 14240-1867
IN CANADA: P.O. Box 609, Fort Erie, Ontario L2A 5X3

Not valid for current subscribers to Harlequin Intrigue books.

**Are you a subscriber to Harlequin Intrigue books
and want to receive the larger-print edition?
Call 1-800-873-8635 or visit www.ReaderService.com.**

* Terms and prices subject to change without notice. Prices do not include applicable taxes. Sales tax applicable in N.Y. Canadian residents will be charged applicable taxes. Offer not valid in Quebec. This offer is limited to one order per household. All orders subject to credit approval. Credit or debit balances in a customer's account(s) may be offset by any other outstanding balance owed by or to the customer. Please allow 4 to 6 weeks for delivery. Offer available while quantities last.

HI11B

*Harlequin® Special Edition® is thrilled to present a new
installment in* USA TODAY *bestselling author
RaeAnne Thayne's reader-favorite miniseries,*
THE COWBOYS OF COLD CREEK.

*Join the excitement as we meet the Bowmans—four
siblings who lost their parents but keep family ties alive
in Pine Gulch. First up is Trace. Only two things get under
this rugged lawman's skin: beautiful women and secrets.
And in Rebecca Parsons, he finds both!*

Read on for a sneak peek of
CHRISTMAS IN COLD CREEK.
Available November 2011 from Harlequin® Special Edition®.

On impulse, he unfolded himself from the bar stool. "Need
a hand?"

"Thank you! I…" She lifted her gaze from the floor to
his jeans and then raised her eyes. When she identified him
her hazel eyes turned from grateful to unfriendly and cold,
as if he'd somehow thrown the broken glasses at her head.

He also thought he saw a glimmer of panic in those
interesting depths, which instantly stirred his curiosity like
cream swirling through coffee.

"I've got it, Officer. Thank you." Her voice was several
degrees colder than the whirl of sleet outside the windows.

Despite her protests, he knelt down beside her and began
to pick up shards of broken glass. "No problem. Those trays
can be slippery."

This close, he picked up the scent of her, something fresh
and flowery that made him think of a mountain meadow on
a July afternoon. She had a soft, lush mouth and for one
brief, insane moment, he wanted to push aside that stray lock

of hair slipping from her ponytail and taste her. Apparently he needed to spend a lot less time working and a great deal *more* time recreating with the opposite sex if he could have sudden random fantasies about a woman he wasn't even inclined to like, pretty or not.

"I'm Trace Bowman. You must be new in town."

She didn't answer immediately and he could almost see the wheels turning in her head. Why the hesitancy? And why that little hint of unease he could see clouding the edge of her gaze? His presence was obviously making her uncomfortable and Trace couldn't help wondering why.

"Yes. We've been here a few weeks."

"Well, I'm just up the road about four lots, in the white house with the cedar shake roof, if you or your daughter need anything." He smiled at her as he picked up the last shard of glass and set it on her tray.

Definitely a story there, he thought as she hurried away. He just might need to dig a little into her background to find out why someone with fine clothes and nice jewelry, and who so obviously didn't have experience as a waitress, would be here slinging hash at The Gulch. Was she running away from someone? A bad marriage?

So…Rebecca Parsons. Not Becky. An intriguing woman. It had been a long time since one of those had crossed his path here in Pine Gulch.

Trace won't rest until he finds out Rebecca's secret, but will he still have that same attraction to her once he does?
Find out in CHRISTMAS IN COLD CREEK.
Available November 2011 from Harlequin® Special Edition®.

HSEEXP1111

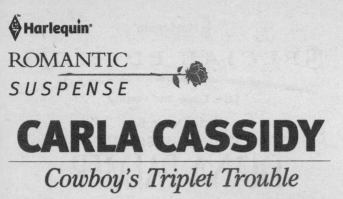

Harlequin®

ROMANTIC
SUSPENSE

CARLA CASSIDY
Cowboy's Triplet Trouble

Jake Johnson, the eldest of his triplet brothers, is stunned
when Grace Sinclair turns up on his family's ranch declaring
Jake's younger and irresponsible brother as the father of her
triplets. When Grace's life is threatened, Jake finds himself
fighting a powerful attraction and a need to protect. But as
the threats hit closer to home, Jake begins to wonder
if someone on the ranch is out to kill Grace....

A brand-new Top Secret Deliveries story!

TOP SECRET
DELIVERIES

Available in November wherever books are sold!

www.Harlequin.com

HRS27751

SPECIAL EDITION

Life, Love and Family

This December
NEW YORK TIMES BESTSELLING AUTHOR

DIANA PALMER

brings you a brand-new Long, Tall Texans story!

Detective Rick Marquez has never met a case he couldn't solve or a woman he couldn't charm. But this smooth-talking Texan is about to meet the one woman who'll lasso him—body and soul!

Look for TRUE BLUE
November 22 wherever books are sold.

www.Harlequin.com

Harlequin
Super Romance

Discover a fresh, heartfelt new romance
from acclaimed author

Sarah Mayberry

Businessman Flynn Randall's life is
complicated. So he doesn't need the
distraction of fun, spontaneous Mel Porter.
But he can't stop thinking about her. Maybe
he can handle one more complication....

All They Need

LONGER
BOOK
Same Price!

*Available November 8, 2011,
wherever books are sold!*

Harlequin® *Desire*

ALWAYS POWERFUL, PASSIONATE AND PROVOCATIVE.

NEW YORK TIMES AND USA TODAY BESTSELLING AUTHOR

BRENDA JACKSON

PRESENTS A BRAND-NEW TALE OF SEDUCTION

TEMPTATION

TEXAS CATTLEMAN'S CLUB: THE SHOWDOWN

Millionaire security expert and rancher Zeke Travers always separates emotion from work. Until a case leads him to Sheila Hopkins—and the immediate, scorching heat that leaped between them. Suddenly, Zeke is tempted to break the rules. And it's only a matter of time before he gives in....

Available November wherever books are sold.